Love, Life and Ambition

Love, Life and Ambition

Give your name an identity

Bharat Agarwal

MAHAVEER PUBLISHERS

Published by
MAHAVEER PUBLISHERS
4764/2A, 23-Ansari Road, Daryaganj
New Delhi - 110002
Ph. : 011 - 66629669-79-89
Fax : 011 - 41563419
e-mail : mahaveerpublishers@gmail.com

First Published: June 2010
Fifth Impression: September 2011

Love, Life and Ambition
ISBN (10) : 8183520103
ISBN (13) : 9788183520102

Distributed by
VAIBHAV BOOK SERVICE
e-mail : vaibhavbookservice@gmail.com

Distributed in Nepal by
BAJRANGBALI BOOK ENTERPRISES PVT. LTD.
Jyatha Mushyabahal, Ward No. 27, Kathmandu, Nepal
e-mail : bajrangbalibooks@gmail.com

Printed by Jaico Printers, New Delhi

Dedicated to

Papa & Maa

Acknowledgement

I am really thankful to that adroit person who had given us the word, 'Thank.' If this word didn't exist, I wonder how I would have thanked all my supporters.

I am really thankful to God, who had given me a permit to come to this planet as a human with all my tangible assets in the right place. I am thankful to my parents who have given me a hale and hearty body draped with their blissful blessings. I am thankful to all the influential mentors of Scindia School who allowed me to take education from them. I am thankful to my publishers—Mahaveer Publishers—who have given me immense support. It is always difficult for a writer to get published in this not-so-lucrative market of writing but my publishers proved that this fact was not true. I am thankful to all my friends who have had vouched for me and told me that I am good enough to write a book. Here, I want to specify the names of my friends who were an indispensable part of my life along the process. And those special names which have made my life prosperous are Ashish Shukla, Chirantan Pawel, Deepak Grover, Hari Om Mishra, Maneesh Sharma, Monson Mathew, Mukul Mukesh, Rajesh Kumar, Rishi Pal, Rupali Jain, Sankalp Agarwal and Vipin

Ponnath. Everything has a beginning and therefore I am highly thankful to the enterprise named IBI Biosolution Pvt Ltd, Panchkula. I went there to get industrial training for six months scheduled by my college, ICFAITech, but only one thing I could do and it was to write with the help of their lab computers. I don't know how but in Panchkula I had the desire of being a writer and I am still on with the same feel.

In fact, I think writers don't write because they can write. They write when they find viability in the world of humans and technology and this viability directly comes from beautiful people and beautiful things. For beautiful things, I am grateful to Nature, which has managed to keep the wonders of the world sublime despite confronting innumerable environmental hazards. And for beautiful people, I simply congratulate all the great Moms who have produced some illustrious personalities like Congress leaders, the king of Bollywood, the US President and many more.

However, I have no wrong intensions in stating that a few of them were in my class too—some had tempting dimples in their cheeks and some had ponytails at the back.

I wish everyone of them would remain with me so long as I am alive.

A Word or Two

How many of us actually know what this material world actually has? If not, then let me tell you that this world has unpalatable humans who are living their intangible dreams with unrequited love.

In this book you will feel the essence of stupendous talent and sublime love that make existence possible. Witness the glorious past which has now been unearthed and the truth which is no longer hidden.

Happy reading!

Bharat Agarwal

(bharat.2103@yahoo.com)

www.bharatagarwal.com

A Vicious Miscreant

* * * * *

We all try to improve our own sagacity to curtail every bit of profanity and do something better, but often we fail to behave as humans. In our bid to reach the pinnacle of success, we resort to unscrupulous means while playing our respective roles. We have become so selfish and corrupt that we hardly give importance to the existence of other human beings. We love to earn millions, but never compute how many times we might have found ourselves thankless and reckless. We try not to plummet, but we generally forget that we are the only reason for this happening. As a consequence, we need a curtain-raiser for ourselves, or a trustworthy person who can really tell us the reality of this grim world.

"Humans are no longer humans," I repeat this again and again, till I find someone less nasty than me.

If someone were to ask whether there is anything which glitters more than gold or whether there is anyone who never gets old, then our answer will inevitably be in the negative. But what I want to point out is that there is something which can impart more shine to us and something make us feel young again and that is our *deeds*.

We might have seen innumerable good and bad things, but now is the time to see something which can stop our heartbeats. A story is somewhat like a sieve which allows all betrayal to stay on top while the rest collects below. It is an indispensable part of a person's life wherein he has been good to others, conscientious in his studies and overall maintained a pleasing personality. This so far unsaid story is like colour which allures you as a reader, or I think, it is a depiction of lascivious happenings in one's life. But who am I to tell you all this stuff, isn't it? Where am I right now? Why am I not coming in front?

So, get ready for the ride, dudes. Leave aside all the hanky-panky things for a while to give full attention to what I have to tell. Let me begin by going back into the bygones. Here I go…

At the Fort

* * * * *

I am at the fort. Right now, I am standing close to the boundary of this huge fort. There is only one step left for me to miss the floor. If I were to take that, then who would tell you the story, dudes? If I were to look down, humans would not be seen. I am at such a height from where I can only see lights blinking in houses, imparting the glitter of twinkling stars in the sky. I am caught in between. But why am I standing like this? Maybe I am finding my life cumbersome?

I am here neither for a night walk, nor am I prowling here. In this pitch darkness, there is no need to think about the stock market, the life insurance plans, education plans or my 'car-home-fees loan'. I am substantially rich and luckily enough, I have not received any threatening calls from my enemies. I am merely wandering here and there to decide whether to jump down from this height of a thousand foot or more or not, despite being in possession of inestimable wealth and fame.

I wonder if my deeds have destined this for me! Should I be more brutal or do I deserve a somewhat lenient punishment? I have already moved in, more than a hundred, to and fro motions from one end to another like a pendulum, but denouement has not come yet. I will keep thinking the same thing till my last breath. But why should I bore you people with my aimless chatter?

Let me clarify this because I believe in the importance of public opinion as it helps many of us, including myself to take quick decisions without any dilly-dallying. So, let me give you the opportunity to decide on my behalf. Be prepared to read every word of this book so that you are able to tell what I should do after you have completed the reading. Just tell me, is there any other way to resettle what I had done?

I have been a person of my own values and have been living on my own terms and conditions for years now. Though I am tempted to wonder where my values have gone, I have invariably relied on the advice of only one person and that's been me only. However, I seem to have lost that person somewhere in this baneful world. Right now I am standing here with my hands empty.

I completed my schooling, bachelors of technology, masters in science, masters in research and Ph. D. Does it not make you wonder if I left anything?

I had my complete education in United Kingdom as it is *the* place where you have a lot of scope to earn a lot of money and that too in sterling pounds. Currently the value of the British pound is 1.5964 US dollars and 1.5964 dollar = 74.2645 INR. This means that even if you earn a meagre amount in UK, you can lead a comfortable life in India. However, I did learn one thing and that is good fame, good money, or both do matter in every phase of life. I believe everyone has to have an optimistic 'desire' to help them to become prosperous and pragmatic. But here again, a question rises and that is, how can such a knowledgeable person be so under-whelmed?

Every one of us is quintessential in one's own world of certainties and uncertainties. What is more important is to have individuality, no matter what it costs for it to be so. Put in your best to make life affluent; keep working as long as possible; remain detached from the rest of the beings unless you need them desperately and be distant from every relation to avoid getting caught in the web of emotional attachment. Just be focused and do what you have been doing for years. This has been my motto in life till I came to this fort for the first time.

Now I realise that remaining focused had its advantages but for how long can man continue thinking about himself and his own world? I am not the only one who is living here and doing work; there are many more like me in this world. I am neither a president, nor a prime minister, nor a chief minister, nor the chief of Army or Navy or Air Force. I am just a normal human being whose normalcy is dependent on some supernatural power. Therefore, it is essential for me to look at others and learn from them how to be a responsible citizen, instead of being selfish and self-centred as I have been. Alas, this thought has come to my mind only when I find myself drawing closer to death.

This change of mind has come rather late. Maybe yours will come after a decade, or maybe after you commit something wrong and have seconds left to feel it. But it always comes in a very subtle manner and it depends on how you take your life, just as it happened with me. Luckily, I had time to realise my transformation and have time left to make amends while making you aware of it too.

After acquiring all my degrees, I switched to teaching as I always wanted to impart something of my learning to all budding scientists. I worked in universities as in-charge of sciences and received a whopping amount of money for it as though I was the only the person doing this. But I enjoyed all that I did abroad. My degrees were so impressive that I was given a hassle-free entry into the research field where I got everything whatever I deserved as a scientist. I helped many Indian students to get admission. I had passed through many departments, from low to high, followed by the higher and the highest. I began my career as a lab assistant; then I became a senior lab assistant, a junior supporter and finally a guest faculty in various universities. I even worked as a project manager and spread awareness among the people on health-related issues. Many research papers were published under my name. Finally I took to teaching as a full-time profession and continued for over 25 years. I started my career at the very raw age of 20. I stayed in United Kingdom right up to retirement before deciding to return to India.

Since I had spent a major part of my life abroad, I had earned enough to spend freely. I could well afford to be lazy now.

I have always maintained that there is no fixed age for retirement, but then I had simply become tired of working there. When I reached India, I had pots of money with me. So I opened my own lab. I began to do my own experiments and projects. I could watch TV, enjoy expensive meals, wake up late and undertake fresh projects. One day, I received an unexpected call from Scindia School asking me to join them, despite not having sent my curriculum vitae in naukri.com.

"Just kidding," I said in my interview that was held in 2004 at Scindia School. I took my interview in a very light vein though I could notice I was being observed very closely. However, I was enjoying all the attention that I was getting. I knew that my experience abroad had given me this chance to be one among the Scindians. I had enough of a reason to say 'no' to them, but I thought it was better to hear them out first.

"You have to guide only one guy out of more than 700, professor," remarked a member from among the panel of interviewers. "Once you say 'yes', we will let you know the details about the work entailed. If you help him, maybe it would help you to earn fame in India as well," they said.

It seemed they had already done their homework. They knew how to entice me.

I became nervous. I had earned more than billions in UK. In fact, the universities and their government had even failed to prove me wrong in whatever I had done.

"Then why the heck are you giving only one student to me?" I asked, peeved at their suggestion.

"This student can be proved bigger than anyone in the UK, professor," said one of the panel members in an enticing tone. "He has been here since long and his entry into Scindia School caused a lot of heartburn among some of the teachers here as well. His performance is unparalleled. His overt as well as covert character is gilded with innumerable qualities. Perhaps you might take some time to realise his qualities, but without any hitch you can make him render any service that you want at any point of time."

"He is almost like you in terms of ken," remarked another.

"However, he can even whittle your problems if you have any," remarked a third, as if he were my father.

My brain had gone awry and I was completely confounded. I felt pressurised and leaned forward to drink a glass of water. Then I waved to a 'helper' to get me a cup of coffee as I felt in desperate need of it.

"What taste would you prefer to have, sir?" he asked gently.

"A black one," I answered as he cast a peculiar glance at me. Surely everyone is entitled to have a coffee at least.

Then I took my own time to ponder over the offer made by the panel, while slipping my coffee slowly and deliberately.

"Can I have the curriculum vitae of the student?" I asked.

"Even I as principal, just as all the teachers, housemasters and assistants of this school can tell you about him as we all have studied his CV thoroughly."

'Good for you,' I thought to myself. But I said, "Well. It's good to hear this, but I need time to think," I uttered importantly.

"Okay, here it is," they said, pushing the CV of the student lying on the table across to me.

"Thank you, sir," said I, taking the paper in my hand.

"You can take your own time. We can wait until you decide, professor," they said in one voice. Their voice seemed to haunt me. It was quite possible that they wanted me to decide in a jiffy, so that the due procedure could be initiated.

"We hope you would like him, Dr Paul Smith."

'Thank goodness, they addressed me by taking my full name,' I thought wryly.

I took the list in my hand and gave a cursory glance at the list of his talents, achievements, awards, activities in school and at inter level. It could easily have filled reams of pages. His CV symbolised the spirit of Scindia. The next few minutes, I spent in admiring the first page only which was filled with designs and colours. I was trying to judge the character of this boy in the hope of 'predicting and winning'.

But I couldn't. I failed to succeed. I heaved a sigh of relief for not having indulged in these kind of games which were often telecast on our television and mobiles. Then I licked my finger before turning over to the next page. As far as the general format was concerned, I noticed his CV was wrongly set. However, I really enjoyed going through every page of his bio-data. For the first time in my life I had ever seen such a resume—a resume which was almost tantamount to a mental shock.

The first thing I noticed at the top of the second page was the name Ayushman Agarwal. His CV contained lots of information to boost any student's morale and it was no surprise that the school always kept a copy of his CV in the library to give an idea about the importance of being Ayushman Agarwal. I was completely enraptured by his qualifications and work.

A few questions must have arisen in you by now, I suppose. You must be curious to find out about the nature of my job. Did I do anything for others? Did I live only in my own world? Is my personality based entirely on fallacious appellations, or is there something credible still left in me?

To obtain an answer, you will need to travel a bit more. So, are you ready to travel with me into the bygones?

A Novice Revolutionary

* * * * *

Tea Centre,
Delhi

Age: eight years, before being sent to Scindia School in 1998.

No one can ever be considered amart around this age, but he was blessed with the ability to exercise superb control over his characteristics as if he knew every part of his mind. He always knew how to run his body and soul in a positive sense; his qualities, his hard work, his speculations, his vibes and his vision never showed wildness. He started behaving as a mature person at a very early stage of his life.

So, now it is time to roll up the curtains and to introduce someone who actually brought down every fence and led us to cerebrate in every field of science and humanity too. Life is all about hard work and here was this boy named Ayushman Agarwal, who gave a new definition to hard work.

Ayushman stood at the tea centre which was close to his house. He was waiting like others to get tea as none was available at home. His mother was in her Mom's house and Dad was sleeping. After a period of long wait, he got his cup and some tea in the kettle. All of a sudden, his eyes fell on a girl standing near and who had been staring at him since he had arrived. He took a sip of tea before looking closely at the girl. He found her smiling he while relished the fragrance of the tea emitting from the steam of the hot tea. Was she enjoying the tea or was she smiling at him? He looked at himself to check if he was dressed alright and found to his relief that all was well. He was dressed as simply as was expected of him. He noticed she was rather fetching to look at but he was failed to take a single sip since hes eyes fell on him. Ayushman wondered what made her to smile, giggling silently as if he was someone inside a cage. Ayushman began to panic, while she continued to smile and take sips form her cup. She was aware that she had made him feel uncomfortable, but she continued behaving as before. He stood mesmerised to one spot as though his feet were laden with lead. He continued to admire her from the corner of his eyes. Every giggle of hers was making him more and more intoxicated. He felt as though he had been chopped into innumerable pieces. He had no choice but to turn away from the shop though her face made him stand rooted to one spot. He felt self-conscious and hoped that nothing wrong would occur. He waited for her to complete her cup, so that he could start on his own. However, she seemed in no hurry to complete her tea, as if deliberately prolonging the procedure. She continued with what she had started—laughing and smiling at him. A shiver ran through him, making him feel weak in the knees. So he took a seat, but couldn't stop looking at her beauteous face which was oozing unquenchable heat. This continued endlessly till Ayushman decided to move away with his kettle. Before he could do anything, she moved out of the shop. She was with her family and left with them, leaving Ayushman fuming at her. Finally he gulped the tea down in a single gulp and asked the shopkeeper if he knew who she was.

"About whom are you talking?" queried the shopkeeper.

"That girl with her family," he said rather tentatively, as if afraid to reveal his feelings. He added, "The one who left just a minute ago with her family."

"Concentrate on your studies, son. These things are not really meant for you till you have grown up."

"Please tell me as it is very important for me."

"Important? Are you crazy? You saw her only for a few minutes and now this has become so important for you."

"I have other things to do as well, sir. So, please, can you hurry up and tell?"

"Do not bother about her as she is not normal. She keeps laughing at anyone she sees for the first time. She has been my customer for a year now. She often comes here with guards to protect her," said the shopkeeper before pursing his lips tightly. "As luck would have it, today you happened to be the first guy."

Ayushman returned home and began to wonder how a mad person could look so attractive and why is it not that we are unable to love them like any other normal human being? Why? Is it necessary to love someone after knowing their mental status only, he wondered.

"Why did you become so late, son?" Dad asked him as he had already got up by the time he reached.

Ayushman told him everything and added, "I kept staring at her as I found myself fascinated by her ethereal beauty. In the end, I returned her smile. All I want to say is that today I learnt how to look at those who want others to look at them."

He then turned to enter his room to complete to his studies. He gave tea to his Dad who seemed speechless at his son's words, probably as stunned as the girl had left his son. He wondered how a youngster like his son could ever have such thoughts and values! After all, he was much younger than the great philosophers and illustrious thinkers, who invariably left others shocked with disbelief, thought his Dad.

However, this was not what had rendered his Dad serious and worried. His Dad's concern was more for his inherent skills and this incident was just one of the many others that he indulged in while at home. His finesse was beyond doubt as if it had been tied around his neck when he took birth. His face exuded shades of credence which always made his surrounding dull and morbid. His attitude helped him to earn blessings from everyone around him. He invariably managed to do things right and the praise for this indirectly went to his parents, who decided to send him to Scindia School. Perhaps such a direction was needed for a boy like him. Maybe it could help him to accomplish his never-ending dreams.

His school turned out to be more attractive and better than he had anticipated. Apparently his school still exists and anyone can be drawn to it as also to the students who study here. It has become an accepted fact that a product of Scindia School becomes highly capable and meticulous in his work. Many names can be cited to describe Scindia's never-ending luminaries. It has produced the actor-brothers, Salman and Arbaz Khan; a band of dynamic brothers, Manmeet and Harmeet Gulzar and many models, TV actors and writers like Anurag Mathur, who has penned the novel, *The Inscrutable Americans*, which describes the comical adventures of a young Indian student, freshly arrived in the United States and many more like him, who leave for greener pastures abroad. Ayushman's father too was an alumnus of Scindia School, so it was expected of him to follow in his father's footsteps. His father wanted to see his child to become a celebrity in any field and therefore Ayushman had been sent to Scindia in the hope that he would make his mark there.

So this is the story of a boy who had a sharp mind, was good in extra-curricular activities and who loved to breathe the fresh air, smell the flowers and go for walks to remain healthy. He always preferred working in open space. On account of his seriousness in study, his parents faced no problems in deciding what would suit him best. He was very young when he was sent to a boarding school in 1998. Generally young boys show reluctance to go to a boarding school and quite possibly, Ayushman might have wondered why his parents had been so hard-hearted to send him to a boarding school, but the decision of his parents proved that they were not wrong in their decision.

Ayushman did cry often to show his displeasure at leaving his parents behind but to no avail. He had no choice except to give in to his parents' decision. It was as if a vial of pain had been served to him to swallow whether you, like it or not. Like any other child, he was timid and worried about things like ragging, loneliness and more. So far he had been Dad's boy at home. His tears failed to make his parents change their mind. Basically every male child in his family had stepped out at the same tender age and therefore what his father had done was nothing new. His parents were however worried about him. They wanted their son to learn things for himself than be told by them. They wanted him to fly high like birds do. It is said that life at home is different to life at a boarding school and it helps to toughen up children. Anyhow, Ayushman was having a similar atmosphere at the boarding school as at home, so much so that his mother used to tease his father by saying, "Scindians are not meant to be at home." She used to tell her son, "Become more than just a Scindian within you."

This story is about Ayushman's life in school. His journey started in 1998 when he was enrolled in Class VI. His stay in school was more of a sojourn of a few years which never came to an end. His life story is not as old as our history, nor is it wide as the sky, nor as dangerous as global warming, nor a fairy-tale like that of Cinderella. However, his story has a lot of charm. His way of life couldn't keep him captive to his surroundings for long. He kept relying on whosoever he met, though he did not get much in this direction. He kept making friends but some of them left him in between, though a few stood by him till the last. He treated everyone as a quintessential part of his life. He joined Scindia School with the aim of earning his Master of Sciences. However, it cannot be said that his stay in school was a bed of roses, but neither was it a path full of thorns.

You will find that his life became a coin which was tossed many times throughout his Scindian life. Is being a scientist so difficult? No one can say with certainty. Only on completing this book will you be able to gather this information.

Entry to Bring Change

* * * * *

Scindia School was founded by the late Maharaja Madhav Rao Jayaji Rao Scindia of Gwalior in 1897. The school earned a name for itself in no time because of its good standard and in developing all-round personality of the students. Even today, the school offers many subject options to help in the growth of the student and aims at making the student affectionate and well mannered. The school is divided in two sections—the junior school and the senior school. The junior houses are guided by housemistresses, matrons and other domestic staff, while the senior houses are mentored by housemasters and a resident tutor along with the necessary domestic staff.

The Scindia School is bifurcated into two sections—the junior section comprises Classes from IV to VI and houses like Dattaji, Jankoji. Nimaji and Kanerkhed; the senior section is divided in two blocks, south and north block and the classes range from VII to XII. The houses included in the south block are Jayaji, Ranoji, Mahadji, Jeevaji, Madhavji and Shivaji; the north block comprises

Daulat, Jayappa and Jyotiba. Both the blocks in the senior section are akin to each other in terms of facilities and guidance, the only difference being that the south block is much nearer to the academic block and north block is some distance away from the academic block. It means that that the north block students have to walk more and leave a bit earlier for every school activity. However, distance hardly matters in a Scindian's life.

The division of the school marks a form of demarcation between the juniors and the seniors and helps to make for a better ambience. If one sought admission to the senior school in August 1998, he was not given the permission to jump to the senior section directly. Everyone had to attend a year or more in the junior section and experience the life in the boarding school before qualifying for the senior section. This was meant to acclimatise the student to the tough life as a student and learn to show respect to seniors. The motto was 'not to defy elders because they are not only old, but God in human form.' In the junior school, the rules were a bit hard to digest while in the senior school, boys enjoyed greater autonomy.

In August 1998, Ayushman's family left Delhi and reached Gwalior fort on the scheduled date. He was accompanied by his parents because it was his first outdoor venture ever. He was quite excited, but timid too about possible things which he might have to face in Scindia. They reached the desired venue where registration was to be done. Thousands of people were seen standing in long queues, waiting for their call to come. Meanwhile his Dad began to recall his own school days and felt satisfied with the growth of the school. He was glad that his son would soon be a part of his own alma mater. The school seemed crowded because of the new entrants and the new admission seekers that year. While the son was trying to establish a bond with the new boys, his Dad was busy meeting the teachers who had taught him during his own schooldays. Both the father and son were on their respective hikes. Registration was almost over and they were slated to attend a party where the freshers or newcomers were to be given the chance to interact with each other and with their juniors and seniors before joining their respective school houses next day.

According to Scindian norms, every student is expected to speak a few words about himself and his expectations on the school stage before venturing into life as a Scindian. It was an opportunity to open out and get the courage to speak in a crowd. Scindia always has such ceremonies in its campus. It helped children to start speaking in front of others from the very first day and overcome their initial inhibitions. Boys had to speak in front of all the parents, housemasters, housemistresses, joint-teachers, class teachers, staff and many more. It seemed as if the students were given the chance to convey to their teachers their views and thoughts.

It was seen that every student was trying his level best to set the stage ablaze in his own style and win over the large crowd assembled at one place. Possibly there were some who thought there was the need for something outrageous to be spoken and this came from Ayushman Agarwal. His name had already been pasted on the notice board due to his success in the entrance examination and thus was known even to the senior boys and the teachers. When his name was announced, a hush fell on the crowd as if awaiting some golden words to drip from his mouth. The crowd stood waiting to hear his words as though he was a President Barack Obama about to give his acceptance speech. Ayushman made his way through the crowd, reached the floor, climbed up, his steps and reached the podium, where he had to make big promises. He was about to make his first speech in front of a vast crowd. His parents could not control their tears, overwhelmed and charged as they were.

Ayushman began, "I am much honoured to see myself on the dais of the Scindia School and wish to say 'hello' to all of you; a big and warm hug for all Scindians, parents, and my new mates who are here for some or the other reason. My name is Ayushman Agarwal but I conceive that this appellation is worth a naught until I append some charm to it. Moreover, I expect that charm to come to me here at Scindia and by being a Scindian only. I don't know what all Scindia School has given to my seniors and to those who have already passed out, but I truly thank the Scindia School for allowing me to be a part of their incandescent family.

"To establish oneself, one needs to have big dreams and potent ways to accomplish them all. I have a bit of both and I hope that Scindia School would help me to develop the rest. I wish to state that I am not expecting everything from this edifice alone as I have been taught that we have to help ourselves first before others can help us. Besides, I want to convey the message to all of you that you need to enjoy here as much as you can. In fact, we all are here to get ameliorated so that we could come out good in the end while understanding the meaning of this world. Just study and have fun."

"Thank you all," he finished and many of the staff started congratulating him as though motivated by his words of wisdom. Ayushman took one step down and half the crowd moved towards him. He descended one further step and the rest of the crowd drew near him. When he was on ground level, he was surrounded by the entire crowd. In his first speech itself, he had managed to attract people and leave an indelible impression on everyone's mind. Ayushman was the first one to be noticed and became well known as an articulate speaker too. Then his parents took leave to retire to their hotel 'Shelter' for the night.

Next day, Ayushman was slated to join his house, the Dattaji house in the junior section. Strangely enough it was the same house to which his father had belonged in his schooldays. It seemed that Ayushman had been given the opportunity by the school to start his life from where his father had left earlier.

The rest of the students, who were new to the school and did not possess any Scindian in their family, were given houses on the basis of a computer-based random process.

Next day, Ayushman's mother's role began. As we all know, mothers are an essential part of life to keep the things hassle-free. The moment she stepped out off the car, her grace and charm rendered the onlookers speechless. While his father went to meet his housemaster downstairs, his mother went up the stairs to take a look at the dormitory and other stuff. She was eager to see where her son would sleep, where he would have a bath and where his wardrobe and his study room would be. She was doing the most obvious things that every Indian mother does for her child. Ayushman, however, was somewhat tense at seeing his mother do all these things. He was relieved that at least his mother had not asked someone about her future daughter-in-law. She started unpacking his bags and helped him to settle down soon. She was busy with him while the others were busy with her as they gazed apprehensively at her. Completely unfazed, she continued doing what she had come for. After all, she was the wife of a Scindian. It was well known that the Scindians always got better wives, no matter how good they were as husbands. After unpacking, she came down and asked his Dad to come out from the housemaster's residence as it was time to leave. Everything had been done except to exchange the goodbyes.

Both his Dad and Mom sat back in their car and waved through the car window at the receding school campus and the occupants. The family could only share a flying kiss before they had to disperse. Ayushman stood solemnly under a tree and kept staring at their car till it disappeared in the horizon. Now an overpowering bout of grief engulfed Ayushman and he began to resolve he would have to manage without them till the holiday for the Raksha Bandhan festival arrived on August 7, 1998.

"You need to learn that boarding schools are meant to keep a child away from the parents for a while, so that they learn to value life and loneliness," said his housemaster while talking to him later on. He also told Ayushman to start life with this lesson which would stand him in good stead later on in life. Ayushman was in school white parents were away from him. He knew that he had to start a new life like his father had started years ago. The only solace was to repose faith in God for the present and for future life too.

Some Demotions

* * * * *

Ayushman was given Dattaji house in junior school where he was needed to survey his life. He was now in his new school where he might get the chance to meet both good and bad. The junior section was at a short distance from the main academic block and some distance away from the senior houses too. He hardly had any seniors in his junior campus and he got the chance to live a peaceful life. But he was not alone over here; more than forty-five boys were living/sharing the same hostel and the same Dattaji house, though there were more students in other houses like Jankoji, Nimaji, and Kanerkhed.

As Ayushamn was not an ordinary guy, he had the maximum number of friends initially itself. Many students were jealous of him too, but then this is an aspect of life only. 'It is a boarding school, so how can you expect someone to be your friend so soon?' Ayushman would tell himself.

Next morning, he was ready to give a 'roll-call' before he left for classes for the first time. It was a normal routine to check how many students actually left for school in the morning. Those who were left behind had to leave for the sick-room, whether sick or not. It was a trend in the school that if anyone stayed behind, then he had to be considered 'frail'. Attendance of these students was taken in the sick-room itself by the doctors. Then both the attendances were tabulated before being forwarded to the almighty of Scindia School and of the thirteen houses—the principal. This system had been carefully maintained though violation of it was common provided the individual had the gall to do it.

After attendance, Ayushman left for his classes with his new-found friends and strangers. His first day in school was very pleasant and overwhelming. He met various teachers, some of whom had taught his father also. Some of the gatekeepers were same too. One said to him, "Ayushman, welcome! Your father used to cross the same gate to attend his classes; now, it is your turn to do so."

Ayushman listened very attentively and he said very politely to them, "Guard sir, I would try to do more what my father did here." He always knew that for being a good person, one has to be a good listener and a good speaker too. Therefore, he always respected one who came to him and encouraged him to come closer too. He attended five periods per day in junior school and the recess began after the third period. The schedule changes on entering the senior section. He enjoyed the first period as it passed very smoothly but from the second period onwards, he found that things and time changed forever.

When the second period began, a teacher with a long moustache, dense beard, tall height and appearing very tough indeed entered his class. His name was Raghav Sharma. "Are you the only guy in this class whose father was at Scindia?" he asked Ayushman, who was seated in the first row.

"Are you guessing, or did you really manage to find out about me, sir?" Ayushman asked in return.

"Someone told me about your appearance last day. In fact, he was very impressed by your speech and told me to take care of you. I am sorry I was absent during your impressive speech as I had fever. So, in a sense, yes, I am guessing."

"Yeah, I am Ayushman Agarwal, son of an old student."

"So can I know your father's name?" the teacher asked.

"Yeah, of course, he is Anil Agarwal, ex-Jayappan, batch of '77," replied Ayushman.

"Good. Next question."

But before his teacher could ask any further, Ayushman blurted out, "Sir, I think I should not be the only person to be asked just because of my family's Scindian background. Why don't you ask something from others too?"

The teacher didn't say anything to him but continued from where he was interrupted, "Good, next question. How do you find the other boys, who are not having any Scindian background, dear? Did you like them?"

"Sir, there might have been many occasions when you must have found your family members different from you, but did you try to identify the disparity among them?"

Ayushman asked impertinently, a bit upset this time. "Sir, this is my first day in the academic block and in my class. I found thirty-two students sitting inside, including my bed-partner (bunk-beds), Anshul Agarwal. I could have sat with him, but I didn't. I decided I will not distinguish anyone on the basis of religion, caste, values, ethics, or Scindian background even. I am not here to make friends, good friends and best friends and so on. I am here to look at everyone equally without being partial. At no point of time did I see them separately; moreover, I found them all alike. I felt there were thirty-two Ayushman Agarwals sitting altogether in one class under one roof, that is, Scindia," said Ayushman. But his answer struck the teacher dumb as he felt here was a student years younger but talking like an elder.

For a minute there was a pin-drop silence. Those, who had not been present at his first speech, got a taste of his razor-sharp tongue.

"Don't you think you are being over-smart? This is what your face has been exuding since the past five minutes," said the teacher in a sharp tone, as if he had been humiliated by a child called Ayushman.

"No sir, I don't agree. There is always a 'feel' behind everything that is spoken. A separate feel exists behind every word, every word we listen, we speak and more. If that feel of performing a 'task' by any individual exceeds the provided limits, then it is called over-smartness, otherwise, the rest is considered smartness only. Moreover, the potent mixture of 'narcissism' and 'infallibility' is known as over-smartness," said Ayushman, "and I firmly believe that I do not have any of these two factors. Therefore I can only be considered 'smart' if you want."

In one breath he carried everyone with him though there were some who felt embarrassed at him. A few students in class were visibly upset because of the tone he had used with his teacher while others were upset as to why they had not said the same things. They were unhappy that why could they not be like him.

"It will be difficult for us to live with him," whispered some of his classmates.

Instead of taking his comments sportingly, the teacher, Raghav Sharma took Ayushman's remarks rather negatively as if someone had landed a hard blow across his face. Feeling somewhat shocked and humiliated, he walked out of the class.

However, Ayushman's reputation spread all around, helping him to make a mark wherever he went. Boys of the junior school started discussing him and despite his raw behaviour, he became a part of the student community in no time. Every boy from the junior section began to mention him with their bed partners at night as if he had cast a fairy-tale impact. But there were a few students who had different plans for Ayushman—they were planning a special treat for him.

He was just like any other greenhorn of his age, but his doings were always enough to leave students mesmerised in class, in school, and in house too. He was so popular among the students that if he had applied, he could have become the principal of the school. Be it his studies or field events, he left his mark behind. His sharp wit and good conduct led his teachers to call him a master.

"Good, at least I have got a new name," said Ayushman to his teachers.

His teachers began to invite him on the dais to give talks on their behalf in Class VI to show others what a young boy could do. Ayushman, even as a child, used to say that you are given a talent at the time of your birth and it only gets better once you start working over it. Obviously he was a minion in front of his teachers, but he could tell others that 'talent is always given in the beginning, but realisation comes when you are ready for it.'

Such invitations by the teachers slowly began to cause ill feelings among the students as they were not prepared to take it any more. Whenever they saw Ayushman speaking on the stage, they directly went to the staff room to complain to the higher authorities. Ayushman was busy setting his mark while the teachers were trying to make the students realise the potential of the boy named Ayushman. Students were considering it a blow to their ego to be shown repeatedly how capable Ayushman was.

"Maybe he is born with some potent desire, but what is it?" his teachers whispered among themselves.

Ayushman never entered into any discussion with anyone and thus no one knew what his desires were. He neither revealed any premeditated plans nor did he share something personal with anyone. It seemed as if he had drawn a veil over his desires, his wants or maybe he was trying to know what he was. He was as much of an enigma to himself as he was for others.

Slowly and gradually, he began to get familiar with everyone in the hostel and in school. Some students became his friends to use him, as politicians do, while most really wanted as a friend. In fact, Ayushman himself never took anyone wrongly and always moved forward to do things with a right approach. He was so impressive that everyone harboured the desire to be like him.

He and his friends started doing a lot of things in unison. He would answer many questions to help his friends in the hostel. This was the only way he knew to settle his adversaries. Whenever he went back to the hostel, he would have long sessions with friends on different topics and on complicated questions. For his friends, he was a master stroke, and for his teachers he was more like Einstein. The teachers were good and the knowledge possessed by Ayushman was incomparable and his concepts unbelievable. Most of the students appeared puny before him. A few students did try to give him a fight, but lost in the end and never tried again.

But things never remain same for long. Change is the law of Nature. There is always a limit to how high one can fly. Moreover, how such a young boy could make everyone revolve around him and this led his fellow beings to plan on his expulsion. Destiny took a wild turn. Some teachers complained about Ayushman's conduct and his deportment in class. On the one hand, they found him capable enough to be whatever they wanted but on the other, they were livid with him. How and why?

The teachers were called for a meeting. The principal of Scindia was persuaded to return to school as he was out of station. By this time, Ayushman had become fully entrenched as a 'nabob' student of Scindia. The teachers felt that because the principal knew him and his family personally, the boy could act so big. This complaint was made by a few teachers and soon it turned into breaking news. Everyone convened at one point. Even the lower staff gathered outside the principal's residence to listen to the verdict and find how a student could be blamed for anything like this.

On September 1, 1998, a meeting was held at the principal's residence. After a while, a very powerful-looking man entered the gate and his car was parked in the parking lot. He stepped out as soon as his car stopped. His driver opened the gate of his sleek Mercedes Benz for him as he was escorted to the meeting room at his residence. The teachers and the other staff stood up to wish him in a loud voice, "Good morning, sir."

It was expected of them to behave thus when facing a prominent person of Scindia School. A meeting which was to decide someone's future was now looking completely aimless as if there never was any intention to discuss Ayushman. The agenda—to take a legal action against Ayushman's irresponsible acts—now seemed as if he was never seen doing anything wrong. A meeting which had to be started with something sober, however, ended with contrary reactions from both the sides.

The principal said, "I have always been called to discuss those who are not performing well. Today, for the first time in my whole tenure, I am called to discuss a boy who is doing so well. Ayushman is even doing better than those who have been here as teachers for decades now."

"Ayushman often makes lame statements and asks unreasonable questions too," remarked a teacher in the meeting.

"He even has to learn how to behave like a student," said another, who was seated next to the first one. The others looked dissatisfied with negative statements and it seemed as if they had always seen him winning glory for the school.

"Statements need to be refined as they are not enough to satisfy us, sir," said R. Mukherjee. He was Ayushman's teacher, who was very close to his student. He was seated across the teachers who had expressed their negativity against him through their remarks like, "Ayushman often comes with futile questions which are not worth answering and disturbs the class on a regular basis. His attitude often generates a feeling of anger among mine students." This was said by the first teacher.

The second teacher nodded vigorously. Mr Mukherjee again came up in the front to protect him. But the truth was that both the teachers were not able to answer his questions in class. They appeared puny in front of the young Ayushman, who too had noticed the discomfiture of these teachers at his questions. Ayushman had already made his housemaster aware about this and the teacher's behaviour towards him. Therefore, their false remarks against a child and their snobbish behaviour towards him got exposed in front of everyone. Happily his housemaster used Ayushman's information to screw odd happenings and remove the opposition directed against the boy. Basically, it was the teachers who were responsible for spreading jealousy and anger against Ayushman.

Verdict of the Principal

* * * * *

"When I work in office, I never look at my watch because I know that time never comes first where the work of this school is concerned. If I devote my whole day, even then I will not be able to complete my work. I have even stopped counting my working hours. Today I came here and kept my work aside. It was sad to see so much of grisly muck and jealousy in your mind for that child. As the principal of this school, I don't need one who cannot gratify a student's curiosity, who cannot fulfil his needs. So, I declare a demotion of both of you—Mr Sunil Jain and Mr Raghav Sharma. You guys should not be seen hereafter in school or anywhere nearby."

Raghav Sharma was the same teacher who had come to class the very first day and had been insulted badly by Ayushman. He was trying to take his revenge along with his fellow companion, Sunil Sharma.

"I will arrange new teachers to vouch for him as every talent needs to be respected in every sense," the principal told everyone present. "I firmly thank Mr Bose for guiding me properly and for telling me the truth. I want to make a short announcement, so nothing should go wrong with him in the future. I am proud to say that I am appointing Ayushman Agarwal as the students' representative (SR) of his batch and captain of junior school. He will remain SR so long as he is here at Scindia School. He will continue to speak from the podium, no matter how he performs," the principal announced proudly.

"Is it fine, Mr Bose, to give this position to your house-boy?" he asked his housemaster in a jovial tone.

"If my house-boy is ready to accept this post, I will be happier than him," replied Mr Bose emphatically.

Thereafter both the principal and Mr Bose kept smiling throughout the day.

End Note

"The meeting is over on a humble note. People who have tried to spoil Ayushman's image are already punished. Ayushman has been appointed as an 'SR' of his batch and captain of the junior school. But he will not remain captain once he enters the senior school, though he will represent his batch even there. He has been given the post of a captain, as he is in Class VI which apparently is the topmost class in junior school. Similarly, this post can be given back only when he enters Class XII in the senior school. If he continues at Scindia School with a similar passion till Class XII, his captaincy will be given back to him," said the meeting organiser at the end of the meeting.

Everything was over and so were the sinister moves. Ayushman was given the most prestigious post in Scindia and the chance to lead his house as politicians lead India. But we always know that every good thing is accompanied with some bad too and the same happened with him. Anyhow Ayushman was not only mentally strong, but also packed with special powers that kept him focused and strong at Scindia School.

Duties

* * * * *

The demotion of two teachers of the school sent a warning signal to others not to indulge in any similar game with Ayushman.

"We just need to help him in every respect in whatever way he wants," decided the teachers.

They all began to help him to perform better and faster in his aim, whatever it was. But somewhere Ayushman's work was earning him criticism. Success always comes with flak. Whenever a guy gets ample appreciation at such a young age for doing something incomparable, then he is bound to attract envy too. Criticism always hurts every person and we need to know how to keep a low profile at this point just as he did. Our elders say our life teaches us everything, but it seems as if Ayushman knew everything from birth itself. He was ready to do whatever was needed before someone else could guide him. It made everyone wonder from where he had learnt all the correct things.

As he was active in studies as well as in extra-curricular activities, he was an idol of many but there were some who could not bear the sight of him. He, however, had all kinds of friends in life and he was curious to know all types.

Students as well as teachers found him doing his work passionately, supporting his house through sports, earning certificates in different categories and confirming his house's reputation in class and his good grades in studies. Indeed he was in a terrific form! You had to name it and he could win it. He fulfilled all his tasks in his own immaculate style.

"Is there any field where he seems weak?" a wanton question that needs no answer.

He seemed to be riding high due to his unblemished work and immaculate behaviour. He seemed ready to do anything required for him and not only for himself, but his friends also. As a result, his friends too did not hesitate in extending their helping hand. As many responsibilities had been placed over him, he needed someone to help him a bit in his work. His good friends helped him as best as they could, but all their efforts went in vain as none of them could match his standard. If Ayushman had to do 100 per cent of the work, then their contribution was merely one per cent of the duties assigned to him. On the other hand, while his contribution to his friends was immense, in return he got nothing. In any case, he never demanded any either. We all come in this world to take our path towards our aim where we need someone to help us.

Let us now talk about his friends—friends who always tried their best to contribute to his life and help whenever he was struck somewhere. His friends on the list according to merit were Aman (a topper since he was born), Monsoon (equal to Aman and very close to Anshul too), Rahul (a hockey player who used to teach Ayushman the same), Rajeev (a sportsman with interest in all the games and filled with tonnes of stamina), Abhishek (the tallest in school and in front of whom Ayushman seemed to be his son whenever they stood together), Gurpreet (the only boy with a turban and an attitude which kept all the mischievous guys at arm's length) and Mukesh Jain (a roly-poly who had to be provided two chairs placed side by side to accommodate his fat behind. His size came in handy when playing football as his body could cover the entire goal when he served as the goalkeeper). There were others too like Rahul, Ashish, Ashesh, Maneesh, Harry and more. There were many more who were like adjuvant for him, so that he could flourish on solid ground too. All of them were good to Ayushman and they all loved to enjoy life with him. In return, Ayushman said, "I know I never look jovial but this is due to my work. Moreover, doing work is like pleasure for me."

Ayushman was so keen to succeed that twenty-four hours never seemed enough for him. He was keen to participate in almost everything and in setting new examples for others to follow. He was a star for everyone. This helped him win many friends but his best friend—who was like a rock, a friend with a firm attitude, a friend with bulwarking nature, a friend with blithesome smile and a friend with bewitching personality—was none other than Anshul Agarwal. Both were so similar that they could be compared to two homologous proteins. There were many reasons for them to share life together. First of all, they were bed partners; the junior school had bunk beds. Secondly, they had somewhat similar gestures, postures, style and personality, so much so that whatever was said of Ayushman applied to Anshul too or vice versa. Thirdly, both had a deep interest in studies and the desire to get their names inscribed in gold. They used to spend their spare time in school by sharing all about life, family, dreams, friends and knowledge.

"Which field do you want to enter?" asked the teachers timidly from Ayushman as the fears of demotion haunted their minds.

"Right now it is better for me to concentrate on my studies alone," he would reply as he had not decided anything till that time. Everyone expected him to become a scientist, but they wanted to hear it directly from the horse's mouth.

"Which way do you want to go in this field, Ayushman?"

"Don't know," would be his reply.

"Are you trying to set your mood first before you tell us this?" the teachers would ask.

"Maybe I am too young to decide anything at this period of life," was his reply.

His school life was running well but suddenly the pressure of work began to take its toll and he fell ill. All his duties and responsibilities had to be put away in the cold storage till he recovered. News of his ill health spread like a virus in school and the delay made everyone nervous as there were dozens of things that needed his attention.

It was the time of a chilly winter. Since the school lay in the fort, it was necessary to keep oneself warm from the cool atmosphere at the fort. Due to long working hours, he didn't attend to his health and therefore fell sick. This happened in the middle of the year 1998. Due to the harsh winter, he couldn't overcome his illness and was advised a long period of bed rest. He was completely bedridden for a month. He fell sick during the mid session and lost out in his studies as well as sports and house activities.

Not good to have bad health, I guess.

"A bad start makes a person liable to face further difficulties. Today I am weak, but tomorrow I may arise again, strong as a bull," Ayushman thought to motivate himself to an early recovery. But his illness made others fly like the phoenix. Everything went wild and his housemates had lots of fun while he was confined to bed. This encouraged the juniors to play truant too and break rules. Student from Classes IVth and Vth became unruly and bold but he was not strong enough to protest even if he felt weak. He came to know that while he recuperated, his classmates were ragging the juniors. He was asleep yet he felt the pain. He tried to muster all his strength to get out of the bed, but couldn't. His desire to save the juniors turned futile. They kept calling out to him for help, but couldn't find any comfort. Later, it became a normal practice in his house as long as he was unwell. A house which was famous for its discipline was now the target of ridicule by all who lost no opportunity in teasing the once-proud 'Dattajians'.

"This kind of indiscipline and devilish behaviour has to be stopped," Ayushman thought. "I have always treated my house as if it was my native place, then how can they misbehave with the juniors when we all are sharing the same roof?"

Every night he could feel the pain the juniors were going through, but he was helpless. He took a couple of days to think what action he could take to put a stop to it all. And then he came out with a solution. The solution was a bit depraving in terms of loyalty, yet he had to resort to it.

Daily they would try to convey to him what they were doing to the juniors. One day, Ayushman didn't react to them. When they drew near his bed, he kept his eyes closed till they all disappeared. He pretended to be asleep in front of them. After a while, he opened his eyes and called out to a junior calmly, telling him to report the matter to the housemaster, so that the culprits could be caught red-handed.

"No," the junior said, refusing to oblige as he feared facing adverse consequences of his act from his friends.

Ayushman reiterated and even added 'please'. The junior asked him, "How can the seniors' request be rejected, sir?"

"Not every time does a student get a smooth platform to perform on," Ayushman taunted him.

Smoothness never brings charm to life, so it is better to keep away from it. Ayushman debated in his mind what to do and said, "I know what to do and what not to do. But I am not left with any other solution except this," he thought.

When this matter was reported to the housemaster, he called all the juniors who had been ragged unduly and summoned the seniors responsible for the ragging. After getting to the crux of the matter, the housemaster reported this matter to the principal. The principal summoned the parents of the miscreants to ask them to take their children back home for a month. This naturally would have affected their grades/marks in the half-yearly examinations.

After recovering from illness and a long hiatus, Ayushman joined his house where he found things back to normal. Everything seemed to be running as smoothly as before. He got a new start to complete the rest of his junior school life. The boys who had been sent home had not yet returned. Ayushman got enough time to settle down and regain his vigour. However, he had to face a lot of negativity from his friends because he had complained about the wrong-doers.

"Good to see my active SR again," said the housemaster on seeing Ayushman back in class. He was welcomed as if he had returned from Mars or Jupiter. His housemaster even gave a party for him and seemed thrilled to see someone who could handle the house better than him. Many of the students waited to get a chance to speak to Ayushman and find out about his experience in the sick-room. Ayushman gleefully replied to the queries of all those who had welcomed him to the party and later all of them got together to have dinner followed by cocktails at night.

Ayushman told everything to the housemaster to save the juniors from getting harassed. At night however, he felt very uncomfortable as he felt guilty at having complained about his schoolmates and kept on debating whether he had taken the right step or not.

Caught in a dilemma he kept thinking, "Am I responsible if their parents got hurt? If yes, then why? I would not have taken this boor kind of decision if they had not behaved as they did with the juniors. Had they been polite, then I surely could have thought of something else at that time. I think use of power is necessary when you have the power. Why should I feel repentant? Everyone's fate is being decided by their own deeds. If they were sent home, then it was their destiny only. They faced this severe punishment because of their vicious wrongdoings."

He dozed off to sleep after contemplating upon all this within himself.

Stupendous Grades

* * * * *

Time to appear for the examinations; examinations which create a sense of fear for all, no matter how well one is prepared or how good in studies. But before we talk about the final examinations for Class VI, let us talk about Ayushman's birthday which happened to fall on March 21, 1999.

His housemaster knew about his dilemma; he also knew that Ayushman was not happy at having been forced to get action taken against his schoolmates. Ayushman was aware of the detached behaviour of some of his friends. In any case he was busy preparing for his final examinations. Though he was elated about his coming birthday, but he was nowhere in a mood to celebrate. On the auspicious day, lots of wishes and love arrived with many wishing him early recovery to good health. Friends from his house celebrated his birthday with full enthusiasm and in the process they got so carried away that they tore Ayushman's clothes too. It was at this juncture that the housemaster arrived and strongly reprimanded them all. He said, "It is good to have you here, guys, but this is the time to attend school. Immediately remove your presence from here till I call you back."

However, the housemaster had a surprise in mind which he later revealed. Ayushman got ready to leave for school to attend his class as his birthday was not a national holiday. He attended every period seriously while others kept coming to his class to wish him, whenever there was a change of teacher. Almost the entire school knew about his birthday. He completed his day and was returning to his room, a bit sad that none of his housemates, the Dattajians from Class VI had attended the classes. He wondered why it was so! It was quite baffling for him and he kept on contemplating over the possible reasons but could not pinpoint any reason for their absence en masse.

"It's my birthday today. I am here, attending my classes, but they all have taken a holiday on my behalf," he thought. He returned to his room and received the surprise of his life. All his mates from his house were ready to celebrate his birthday with a big cake occupying the pride of place. He rushed to the bathroom to refresh himself. When ready, he came out as everyone waited impatiently for him to cut the cake. With a smile spread from one corner of his face to another, he entered and all the boys stood up to admire him, looking swanky in his new black suit which was gifted to him for his birthday.

"Dear, take the knife and give a piece of cake to all in the gathering," said his housemaster to Ayushman.

"Before I cut the cake, I want to say something on my birthday."

Everyone stopped talking and left everything aside to pay attention to what he had to say. A sudden silence enveloped the room as everyone wanted to hear what he had to say and not miss a single word of his.

"I have had lots of memories of junior school as though it all happened not so long ago. I have a vivid picture of every incident that has occurred here. Some were as expected but the rest happened by happenstance only. Everyone knows about them all. Over the months at Scindia School, I have learnt how not to pay attention towards unpleasant things and therefore I never can recall anything that has happened earlier. I really didn't expect that such a celebration had been planned for me. I can say this is one of the best things to happen among all the unexpected occurrences. Though unexpected, it will always remain etched in my heart for years to come. Thank you very much for making me so happy and feel like a birthday boy," he concluded and stepped ahead to cut the cake on the table.

He cut the cake while keeping a pleasant smile on his face. Some of his friends clapped while the rest surrounded him to present gifts, other than what he had already received in the morning too. Some of his friends went to the extent of covering his face with the icing on the cake while some enjoyed licking the same cream off his face. Later, the rest of the cake was distributed fairly among others. Students, who seemed dull and placid in class, now seemed bursting with joy and enthusiasm. It was surprising to from where they could manage to garner all their energies to battle for their share of the cake.

Getting back to his exams, Ayushman did well and in no time the papers came to an end. In fact, he didn't give a chance to the others to feel that he had just completed his papers. Not for a moment did his interest flag while giving his examinations. He was so good that teachers used to correct his answer sheets while standing beside him in the examination rooms. He won laurels for his papers and his teachers were relieved to find the same fire in him which they had seen before he fell ill. The news of his good results was on everyone's lips. He was indeed the most deserving candidate to become a 'master' in not one field, but in all the sciences.

This was the time of his final-term examinations held in May 1999 before his summer vacation was to start. He, as a student, never claimed to be infallible, but his performance was unpredictable to predict. He was an outstanding personality who made others look puny. There was a time when Scindia had some boys who would become silent due to home-sickness, but now even they could be seen talking about him only. He was discussed during morning prayers, breakfast, classes, lunch, games, evening prayers, studies and dinner.

"What kind of a platform can be given to him? What would be best for him? What can suit him better?" asked the teachers while checking his copies as Ayushman had already become the best they had seen.

As his talent came to the fore, everyone had Ayushman's name on his lips. In fact, those who never wanted to be seen with him were now having to hear the comments of the hoity-toity bystanders regarding Ayushman. He became so popular that while some boys began to spread canards about him, the housemasters of the senior school fought to get him in their houses somehow or the other, as now he was known in the senior section too and everyone was keen to exploit his talents to the hilt.

Everyone's result was declared. His answer copies in every subject including Sciences, Hindi, English, Maths and Social Sciences were sent to the principal's office as he was the only student to score 100 per cent marks in all the subjects. The principal went through all his papers lying on his desk and wondered what could be done next! After a deep breath, he sent a notice to all his teachers and it ran as follows: "It is a happy moment for me as a principal to see someone scored marks like this but it may give the impression to outsiders that we have lame examiners in school. They do not know Ayushman as we all do. I feel we cannot give him these marks until everyone knows about him properly. This is indeed a wrong thing to do, but I cannot do anything else. However, he is receiving every kind of scholarship as a Scindian and paying almost no fees to the school. He is a great guy in everything he does and would remain so in the coming years too, no matter what we do with his marks. There is nothing in this world which can stop his success unless he does not want it that way himself."

The principal had gone against all principles to announce amendment of his marks—slight adjustment in his marks. He justified this by saying, "We are only trying to show him as a good student; however, the school will always keep all his original marks as records with them," said the principal in a meeting.

At his request, the teachers made changes in his marks. Though it was illegal to do so, but they did it. However, this unfair act didn't make any difference to Ayushman's life. In fact, this helped him to relax more as it gave him the feel of being a 'topper among rest'.

"Not a bad tag to receive," said Ayushman to himself.

But he had to face the flak at the same time. His critics were not happy to see him with what he had got; they would have been happier if only the marks had been worse. They began to disturb him at the end of the term, but he kept quiet. He knew that as an SR, he had to be more descent. He neither complained to his teachers nor did he say anything to them. He maintained a stoic stance in the face of every adversity. He believed in the adage 'Silence tears anger'.

Then came the long summer vacations for the Scindians as the final exams were over. The seniormost Class VI of the junior section was told to rejoin school after the vacationsz on time. Their vacations lasted till August 1999. After a long and hectic summer vacation, they all returned to school, rejuvenated by the break from studies. The final results had already been sent to the boys. Only Ayushman's results had been announced before time as his copies had been checked first of all. Therefore, he could enjoy his vacations with no tension in mind about the results. He neither studied nor did he stay back at home. He went on a tour of different cities. He enjoyed his life and returned home only a few days prior to the completion of his summer vacations.

The students came and attended the last day in Dattaji house. He and his mates waited eagerly to know which senior houses had been allocated to them. Ayushman was highly punctual and so were his other mates.

Every Dattajian waited with anticipation for the housemaster's arrival to hear the results of those who had failed in the finals and had to reappear for their papers during their vacations. After announcing the results of those who had to reappear for their examinations, he encouraged them by saying every failure is a stepping stone to success but in their case all the failures had been passed.

"Are they really capable of studying in a higher grade? Anyway, the school has shown mercy to them," thought Ayushman.

Mr Bose asked everyone to leave for their senior houses after checking their allotted houses on the notice-board. According to school practice, Ayushman Agarwal again got his father's house, Jayappa house, in the senior section. Before he dispersed, he decided to have a last word with his housemaster. He thanked him and told him how he would forever cherish the memories of the time spent during the one year of academic session in junior school.

The housemaster reciprocated, "I've never had a student like you. Your output has invariably revealed your devotion and concentration in your work. I hope you will maintain it in future and do better still. Ayushman, always remember now that you are not you; you are a boy who joined Dattaji and who has been honed well for going to the senior school. You need to show the same passion in the senior section as well. You need to be vigilant there as you may have to face antagonism some of your classmates. Maybe you will be given fair hours to spend and maybe everything will work out well for you. Anything can happen there. Therefore, be ready and keep doing work. If you fail to do so, then I will be castigated by all. And if you win, then that win will be yours entirely." At this point not only Ayushman, even the housemaster became emotional and both stayed silent for a while.

Ayushman recalled his first day of school life in Gwalior when he stood under a tree while his parents were leaving. Then also, he had been given a similar kind of advice on how to start his life at Scindia School. Now, it was his housemaster who was telling him to work consistently and conscientiously in senior school. He was grateful to his housemaster for guiding him so well all along. He entered the bus, cast a quick glance at everyone, kept his bags near his legs and settled down in his seat. He looked out of the window to wave at him, till the housemaster was out of view as his parents had been when they had left him behind in school. The situations were similar, but the guardians had changed.

August 1999

* * * * *

He was nervous when he joined the senior school. He felt as a toast feels inside a cup of tea—a 'soggy feel'. On discovering that he had joined Jayappa house, his housemates felt disappointed as they felt they would have to compete with him who already was head and shoulders above them all.

He was the master of everything and he always managed to draw a crowd with his witty remarks and prompt answers. He left an impact wherever he went in the senior school too. The senior school's teachers started to enjoy having him just as the junior school had done before. He drew a large crowd of followers in Jayappa house as he had done in Dattaji. He had a good housemaster, green environs, good location, large basket-ball court, a stadium, hockey field, swimming pool, squash courts, horse-riding fields and much more. But all this came along with having to deal with some very rude seniors. When he was in junior school, he was happy not to get any senior as he was the seniormost and a captain too. But now the tables were turned on him. Now he had to deal with students of Classes XI and XII and what a handful these seniors could be! They were like those kings and rulers about whom one had read in history books. Now, such bestial kings were right in front of him and he had to face them as there was no way of avoiding them. He was not the only one to be promoted to the senior school. There were ten more who too had been promoted to Jayappa house as he had been. More than a hundred students were distributed among the other houses of the senior school. He had Classes VIII, IX, X, XI and XII over his own in Jayappa. He was only in Class VII and as per the rules, he had to give over his captaincy though he was still SR.

While everyone of his age-group/batch was enjoying his new house, Ayushman went to check out the academic block as both the junior and senior sections had different academic blocks. In the evening he came back to spend time with his new friends.

The story of his first day doesn't end here. As Ayushman was a big name, he had plenty of guests waiting in his house to welcome him. He had to give his interview in front of his seniors as well as his batch-mates in Jayappa house. He not only had to face the twenty-one seniors of his house, including the Classes XI and XII students but also those who belonged to different houses and who were keen to see who he was. Everyone had to say a few lines about themselves. He was singled out to be the first speaker, maybe because his seniors had no time or maybe they were not keen to have others, or maybe he was the only one who paid his fees. His name was announced first. They said, "So, tell us about yourself, Ayushman."

"Sir, I haven't done anything except to be at the top so far in my life," he replied with utmost simplicity.

"Enlighten us with what you have done," suggested one of the seniors as they were keen to know about his life and how he was like what he was.

"Since childhood I have been scoring 99% or above as 100% was not allowed there as well as it is not allowed here. And whenever I scored so high, my marks were rechecked. My percentage invariably remained high and I haven't had to pay for my studies so far and am not paying here even."

"Then what does your father do with his money?" asked a senior impudently.

"Spend on the other family members while the rest goes for the benefit of the underprivileged children. My father runs a joint venture with many NGOs, like CRY to help others," replied Ayushman. He continued, "My previous school's principal told my parents that I could join them in whatever capacity I liked after completing my graduation."

"Don't worry, no one is going to offer you the same here," retorted one senior.

"I know all this sounds like blowing my own trumpet but it is a fact," said Ayushman.

This information somehow did not go down well with his seniors who began to exchange meaningful glances among each other.

"I want you people not to taunt or provoke me. Let me remain just as I am," Ayushman added.

"How do you manage to be so meticulous despite seeming so ordinary?" asked one of his seniors.

"Do you really think that a guy like me can ever be an ordinary person?" queried Ayushman. "I am blessed. I am told to do a job and I am here to do great things."

"Who said so?" queried his seniors, somewhat rankled.

"This should not be your question, I think. You should only know that when I earn fame due to my work, then I will go back from where I have come."

"From where have you come? And who has sent you? Are you like us or someone else?" his seniors asked, somewhat castigated.

He kept shut as if a wrong question had been asked.

"We guess you must be having a puissant desire behind all this hard work," they remarked.

"Yeah, it is to search myself."

"Why did you chose to join Scindia, if you only wanted to search your name?"

"Firstly, it is my father's old school and secondly, I reckon it will give me a knowledge of things which I can use in my work."

"Like?" his seniors asked.

"Like knowledge, support and love. It can be more than these three also," Ayushman added.

They then asked him to stand away from their crowd since he claimed to be different from the rest. His friends then felt as if they were being treated as outcasts in front of a giant name, Ayushman Agarwal.

In fact, his sledge-hammer performance and fetching smile had been noticed by everyone in the senior school. Before he could start on his senior life, he had promised himself to be always humble in front of all his mighty seniors. Now he decided to behave as an insignificant person in front of them, so that they could get some satisfaction at his incongruity.

Girl in Love

* * * * *

Senior life started. Everyone said that as a senior, you could do whatever you wanted but for Ayushman it merely meant being a student. He was neither ragged to give his introduction nor did anyone dare to do anything with him. His school gave admission only to boys but the daughters of the school teachers could study here.

He was about to attend his first regular session in senior school as everyone waited with bated breath for his arrival. A palpable excitement could be felt in the air. All eyes were focused on him. Everyone had come to attend the class just to catch a glimpse of Ayushman. It was a good chance for those who had missed him the previous night. He entered the building, took out his card, passed it through the machine and even the guard gave a smile when he read the name Ayushman Agarwal popping up.

"I have heard a lot about you, sir," said the guard, who too had heard of him from his colleagues in the junior school.

He smiled to him. He walked ahead towards the notice-board to see his time-table before going to the first floor directly via the staircase to attend his morning classes. Every floor did have a railing for the sake of safety. It was no surprise to find boys diving into a pool, playing cricket, juggling with a ball, studying in the garden, preparing for other activities. When the morning session got over, a crowd of boys could be seen rushing out from their classes in fluttering colours of Scindia. He stood there for a moment and absorbed a real view of a few things, thinking, "I am grateful to Scindia for taking me in." He then entered his class. Ayushman looked relaxed, overwhelmed and cheerful and it was this complacency which riled someone no end. A girl was seated in the front row of the classroom (she was a teacher's daughter) and she saw him first. She had long hair tied with some kind of a ribbon but the left portion of her hair kept falling downwards over her shoulders. She had thin eyelids, wet lips, effervescent voice, jocular face, short height and a slightly attractive glow across her face. This so defines skinny girl fell in love with him and her name was Anamika Agarwal.

"How did it happen?"

"How could a Class VII girl fall in love like this? It is yet to be explored. If you could find out the reasons, then do tell me," said some boy. Anyhow, according to a survey conducted by the *Times of India* of March 29, 2009, love at first sight can occur in just 8.2 seconds.

Here it happened at the time when he placed his first step inside his classroom. It seemed as if she was waiting for him to enter only. Both of them were given the same class. Maybe destiny was responsible for all this. As everyone knew, Ayushman, because of his spotless work career so far in school, he had not faced any problems in giving his introduction to his teachers. Everyone seemed to be talking about him only. instead of their respective subjects. The teachers were happy to see him and so were the students, except for those who hated his guts.

"How could you manage to score so much in your last papers in junior school?" asked some. Many others bombarded him with queries like:

"Who all are your friends?"

"Who is the best teacher here?"

"What did you feel after your marks were modified?"

"Any particular plans for here?"

Ayushman sat silently in his seat. He had decided not to speak but he was forced to as the pressure was building up. After he had heard all the questions, he decided to answer in one line, "What can I say? Maybe I am meant to do this only."

It seemed as if he was attending a press conference before he could finally launch himself in the senior school.

But what is 'love' doing in this scientific story? Is love always needed to score high?

Maybe this was ordained in his life and in hers too. However, he was completely unaware. It was an unusual thing that occurred that time. How could this girl fall in love without knowing Ayushman personally?

No one can describe it because 'love at first sight' is hard to describe in terms of words. It can only be understood as it is something to be felt. What all she had seen in him? What had she felt How did she get attracted, only she could tell. On his part, Ayushman had a blank look on his face when he entered his class. Then what made her to fall in love with him? How could this girl name Anamika take only a few seconds in deciding that she liked him? Either she was completely desperate to have someone as a time pass, or she really thought he was the Mr Right for her.

Ayushman was completely unaware of her feelings and neither did Anamika tell him anything, but many a times she tried to draw closer to him. But Ayushman didn't notice anything in her. Maybe he was not interested at all. As of now, Anamika wanted someone with whom she could share her desires and Ayushman wanted someone whom he could rely on as a friend.

Anamika had found her love in him, but Ayushman didn't find a friend in her. And this war of feelings continued for months. She strove hard to display her feelings for him and at the same time did not want to hurt him as she hardly knew him personally. She proceeded very slowly, as slowly as the earth moves around the sun. She knew what to do and what not to do. She always kept a leash on her actions so that nothing could be taken amiss or could go wrong. There was nothing in common among them except for their dedication towards their respective work. Ayushman was superbly talented in science-oriented work, whereas Anamika was not far behind. She also knew the mantra to get what she wanted and that was Ayushman.

Whether it was true love or infatuation was too early to tell. We even cannot say that it was Ayushman's popularity which made her commit something which she had not expected. She came after one whole year when Ayushman officially joined Scindia School. She didn't even know what he stood for and what all he did at Scindia School. Possibly it was Ayushman's charm which made her fall for him. Ayushman had different ways to solve twisted brain-teasers. Similarly, she did have a lot of new ways to get him. She was so impatient to get him that she made a separate copy about Ayushman. She had Ayushman as the subject in the subject column. She used to write about him: His good and bad angles, his likes and dislikes, his friends and not good friends, his girlfriends (if any), his subjects, his records, his home, family, siblings, how he was brought up in so many years, what he wants from life, and who all desired him as she did. She was mad and getting more mad with every passing day.

Unbelievable how a girl could be so desperate to get someone whom she had never known! She thought that to entice a person, it was necessary to have knowledge about the person. She used to find information on him as if she were a 'Google' engine and slowly started using information to increase her proximity to him. She pretended she knew him well because of the information she had gathered over the months. Her information helped her to become a part of him. For her, they were one body with different feelings within.

If girls do not want a thing, then no one can make them do that thing; but if they want it, then no one can stop them from doing it. Ayushman was happy to find a person who knew so much about him. But he did not know how she knew so much about him. He never tried to find out even. He moved with the flow. Anamika's enchanting behaviour and fetching smile helped her to come closer to Ayushman and the latter relished the way she treated him as a friend.

Gradually both became good friends and she didn't give him any clue at any point of time about her desire to stand by him through thick and thin. Girls exactly know where to hit—coming together, sitting together in class, having lunch, making fun of others and sharing in unison. It all became a part of their lives. Ayushman was so tired of his hectic life that he enjoyed this diversion. A spark had ignited between them but they were the butt of jokes among the students.

"Why should everything be for him—he is a topper and has even taken away the best girl?" glared some of his mates as he passed by.

Anamika had chosen him to fill the gap between them as lovers while Ayushman wanted someone to break the monotony of his life of a recluse. Now they could be seen together everywhere, sharing every moment of their life pleasantly. At times it seemed they complimented so well with each other as though the Creator had made them deliberately as they were. However, this oneness began to make Anamika rather possessive about him. She was in

Class VII, but her desire to get the man of her dreams was beyond limits. Nevertheless, she exercised control over her feelings. She patiently waited for the opportunity to declare her desire openly. In order to get to know more about him, Anamika started meeting every teacher who had taught him in junior school, every friend who had vouched for him and visited every corner of the fort where Ayushman had been with his friends. They came so close that whenever their school would get over, Anamika would offer to drop him to his place. She looked forward to this as she now could say all that she could not do in class. One evening an unpleasant incident occurred. They were sharing information on each other's families and after Ayushman had completed his side of the story, Anamika's face revealed that she already knew all that he had told her. But when Anamika had completed her story, Ayushman was surprised to know such a lot about her. Somewhat Anamika got carried away and complained that Ayushman did not know anything about her till she had told him. She asked tersely, "What do you know about me?"

"You are a girl," said Ayushman in a light vein.

"Well, thank you, but I am trying to find out something else."

"Right. Listen dear, you are a loveable girl and the best friend of mine. Now what more do you expect me to say? One more thing I know about you is that you are a kind of daughter of some kind of teacher."

"Who is that some kind of teacher, Ayushman?" she asked.

"So foolish of me. Who is she/he? I wonder why I didn't ask this!" thought Ayushman, feeling awkward at his lack of curiosity.

"I am the daughter of Anuradha Agarwal, who teaches English in Class X."

"What? How the hell I didn't know this?"

"Ayushman, you never asked me. Anyway, it's not the end of the world, is it?" said Anamika. "I think you also do not know that Arjun Agarwal is a brother of my mother."

"What does he teach? Let me guess. One second. Hmmm, Arjun sir is in the physics department, I think,"

"Right," said Anamika, "and he will teach you physics in Class XI."

Ayushman looked dumbfounded for a moment and blurted out, "So, am I a friend of a person whose mother is going to be my English teacher and whose uncle will be my physics teacher?"

"Yeah, you are cent per cent right."

"What else can I pray for? It seems your entire family is here," he remarked simply. "Is there anyone left who is not here?"

"We all decided to come together," she said. "Both of them applied together."

"How come that all of you have come here? Don't you have any family business?"

"I don't know. I don't know as I am confused," she said.

By now nothing like 'private' was left in their lives, yet she did not reveal particular one secret about her family.

Every minute they were seen spending together and their relationship got further strengthened.

Ayushman, when he entered the senior school, had neither a beard, nor a moustache, nor hair on his chest. He was neither fair, nor muscular in body. His only sex appeal lay in his hair-cut and red lips. These were apparently the most stylish things about his physical structure. And one thing which was like a powerful punch against everything else was his 'mind'. But now, with passing time, he seemed to be changing quite a bit. He was now the least stylist and more attentive towards his work. His red lips had faded now and his black hair had turned grey. What else could one expect from a scientist? It seemed as if whatever chemicals he was using in the lab were affecting his health.

Anamika was lucky in one way and that is she had nothing to fear from any other girl because there were only two girls at that point of time in Scindia School—one was Anamika herself and the other, it so happened, that Ayushman had even failed to notice her. But how long could a person be kept unaware about it, Anamika thought? "Love is needed in one's life but one also needs a lovely heart to feel lovely feelings," Anamika thought. "But how can one fall in love with a scientist who is never aware of his appearance and I think that is why love is blind."

They had already become very close but Ayushman never tried to give any other name to their relationship except that of a 'friend'. She was not interested in anything else except in looking after him. She even started visiting his dormitory which was not allowed. On being questioned, her reply would be, "As I am daughter of a reputed teacher, Anuradha Agarwal, I do deserve this much of advantage."

Even Ayushman couldn't curb this habit of hers.

Such behaviour on Anamika's part was making Ayushman embarrassed and though his friends did not like it, they refrained from saying anything, knowing that he was a decent boy. He would tell his seniors, "She is good and above all, she cares for me."

For Anamika, Ayushman was like a hidden treasure. She was happy being a friend of him and did not want to let him go. But her madness was making Ayushman a bit amused. "We are just friends only, but how can someone be as obsessive as she is?" Ayushman asked himself.

And she started disturbing him during his working hours also. "I am a topper, popular, nabob, SR and a future captain too. So I need to study to maintain my standard. Is it right on my part to devote so much time to Anamika?" he asked himself. "Anamika seems to be getting top priority in my life. If I keep concentrating on her, then maybe I won't be able to go to London for my further studies."

So, one day he made it clear to her about his pending work. But it was too late for him to do so, as she had already lost control over her senses.

Ayushman started concentrating on his studies and began devoting his maximum time to himself. He curtailed the time he devoted to her earlier though they continued to talk to each other. Little had he realised how it would hurt Anamika, who started moving around like a sullen robot.

Anamika had already entered his life very seriously and he didn't have any other option but to humour her along with other things. He wanted to maintain equilibrium in his life. He had however anticipated this outcome and was prepared to face it later. Scientists always speculate well and so could he.

Astonishing Cricket Talent

* * * * *

When Anamika noticed that Ayushman was often ignoring her due to his work, she began to complain, "What we can expect from life is happiness, Ayushman."

Ayushman knew very well that as a human he was allowed to have a life apart from his studies, but the pressure of work did not give him time. He knew he had a dazzling girlfriend, but his work was the topmost priority. When she noticed Ayushman ignoring her, she resolved to keep herself within limits. She somehow curbed all her childish behaviour and began to show maturity in order to draw his attention.

Girls are girls and they know very well how to keep their man happy, Anamika reckoned. But their life was a bit confused. Ayushman was looking for better direction while she waited for Ayushman to re-enter her life. Ayushman had to give time to both work and Anamika, but Anamika had just one work—to spend time with Ayushman. Thus, they continued to meet, but just to keep the relationship going. It was nothing more than this for

Ayushman. They were sitting, going and coming together, but the closeness was missing. Anamika learnt to digest this as she did not want to enforce any restrictions upon him. Every Saturday and Sunday, they started going for short walks so as to rejuvenate themselves. On weekends at Scindia, students tended to revise their whole course of one week, but these two were found strolling in the campus. Ayushman was committed towards his work only and had fixed timings for his studies. He had no interest in doing other things, but he did spare time for Anamika.

You could expect him to do what NASA (National Aeronautics and Space Administration) and ISRO (Indian Space Research Organisation) can do, but you could not make him to fall in love with anyone if he did not want. Whatever he was doing was like what the common man does at the age of 40, and whatever he was not doing was like what we never miss till we get 40+ or keep doing until we last.

"I will have to suffer till he himself comes up and says I love you. Some dreams get fulfilled at the right time, whereas some take more time. I became his friend too soon; he is not my lover yet," thought Anamika as if some premonition told her that her dreams would not be easily accomplished. Things were moving at a steady pace but her expectancy was moving far ahead of time. After all, apart from giving attention to her, he was expected to perform well in class, and at least be average in sports. His housemaster expected him win the cricket trophy as well and told him that he was the lucky mascot for Jayappa house. "Enough of studies we have had from you," said the housemaster to him as he now wanted him to be on the field.

Everyone wanted him to try his hand at all and sundry things. Very high expectations were putting too much pressure on him. This was entirely due to his name and fame. How could Ayushman blame anyone for all this? In any case he loved to play cricket but he knew how to bat only.

"Can anyone be kept away from sports?" asked his housemaster, trying to provoke him into action on the field. "How can someone forget the magic of such a game which is universal?" he added.

There was a second reason too for Ayushman playing cricket and that was Anamika's love for cricketers. He thought if he invited her, then maybe their relationship could go far. He thought he had better start putting his finger in every pie to cover all the potholes between them. Maybe a game could do what a banal human couldn't.

Every house match was scheduled to be held at the Madhav pavilion where a huge crowd was expected to prod their favourite teams on. Everyone loved the way in which the students participated in the league matches and therefore waited with bated breath for the occasion to arrive. What one wanted was to watch different teams, highest run-makers, highest wicket-takers, team with the maximum wins, team with the maximum losses, managers and coaches. None was able to predict either the winners or the losers; all they could do was to speculate.

"Who will lift the trophy?"

"Can the other team make it?"

"Will Jayappa house emerge as the clear winner?"

As it is the cricketers played very unpredictably in a game that was even more unpredictable. The spectators decided to cheer both the teams as both were equal in the game. On the one hand, Ayushman's team-mates were encouraging each other rather than criticising their past performances, while on the other, the opposing team was trying to identify the weaknesses and shortcomings of their adversary, so that they could exploit the weaknesses to convert them into their victory.

"You have to be bit swift on the field while playing," said his captain in an effort to motivate him.

"Don't forget to punish the loose balls," advised the captain of the other team. "Hit hard for a six; run between the wickets to take cheeky singles."

"Don't miss the balls landing outside the off stump."

"Don't play in haste in the beginning of the game and don't waste balls at any point of time."

Ayushman invited Anamika to come as a spectator to witness the thrilling match and encourage him. She was given a seat near the boundary line as she had to be close to him. She also felt that maybe her presence would prod him to put in his best.

The match began with a win for Jayappa house in the form of the team captain winning the toss and they elected to field first. However, the crowd was getting restless to see the teams on the field and that only made the game hotter. Ayushman chose the boundary for fielding; it served two purposes—one he could see her, second, he could even talk to her in free time.

"Wonder, where the devotion to the game goes when a player sees a cunning beauty nearby?" his housemaster uttered, when he saw Ayushman talking to Anamika.

Finally the match got over with 196 runs scored by the other team in 30 overs. Apart from the drama on the field, another drama was being enacted near the boundary. Ayushman was found talking to Anamika as soon as the first session started. He was therefore kicked off the field. He even missed to halt the speeding ball at the boundary due to his inattentiveness. He was told to be a fielder, but he chose to be a chatterbox while the game was on. As he could bat only, he didn't show any interest in his fielding. He ignored his responsibility and even forgot that he had to be alert on every ball, no matter what all he knew about the game. As he was kept out, the twelfth player was brought in to field.

Now it was the turn of Jayappans to bat and Ayushman was sent in as the the opener; he had been included in the team for the same purpose. He was provoked into action when he inadvertently overheard some of the students saying that all he was good in was studies. He was recalling all those victorious moments which he had missed when his house had won while he was busy studying. He was remembering what all had gone wrong between him and her. He could not forget how badly he had fielded. He was thinking about all those extra runs which he could have saved, had he been more alert. He was visualising how he would celebrate if his team won. Before the umpire could start the second session, Ayushman had already decided on what he had to do and how.

The umpire dropped his hand, allowing the bowler to bowl. The bowler ignited himself and started running—slow in the start, mid-slow in between, fast in the end, and super fast before releasing the ball to him. Ayushman wore a tense look when he saw the bowler coming towards him, but he knew how to act. As soon as the bowler released the ball, it bounced so high up that it reached far above his head. The bowler looked satisfied on noticing the signs of fear in his opponent's eyes at the oncoming bouncer. It was above his waist length. Luckily for him, Ayushman was quick enough to intercept the ball and before the umpire could raise his finger to signal something, the ball was already in the crowd without being tipped into the fence. On his first shot only he had rendered service for what he had been sent first. The bowler, who was looking satisfied a minute ago, now wore a harassed look. The umpire took out his left hand for the no-ball and then raised his fingers up into the air to signify a 'six'. The crowd stood up to shout and scream. Ayushman felt fully pepped up. Jayappa house started their score with a six with the help of that player who had been sidelined for more than two hours. Now there was no stopping Ayushman. His bat seemed to be meant for punishing the ball. While his bat hit out at the ball, the runs kept piling on the score-board…

He scored an unbeaten 103 in just 96 balls in the second session. He was egged on by his friends, his teachers and by everyone who were witnesses to his breathtaking knock. Anamika clapped at every run that he scored on the field. He had made the task so easy for his team-mates that they could easily chase the huge score put up by the opponent. It was a historical coup for the Jayappans in the finals ever played on the Scindian pitch.

Scores:

Team one: 196/10 in 30 overs.

Jayappa house: 200/5 in 25 overs.

With this century, Ayushman became the highest run-maker in the entire tournament as his score in all the four matches was huge. Next morning, in the assembly hall (where morning prayers and announcements take place), Jayappa house was declared a clear winner in the tournament. Every player stood up from his seat to receive the trophy as Ayushman Agarwal led his team. He was awarded a special gift for his contribution to cricket played on home pitches. The special prize was a long golden bat placed inside a mirror box, with 'Scindia' written on the lid and his name on the front side of the bat. He dedicated his award to his friend Anamika and to his house too. He had shown that even a bookworm could do wonders on the field.

"I won this trophy because my housemaster had reposed faith in me and felt that I could do it," said Ayushman, while receiving accolades from one and all.

His victorious innings made his house proud of him. After their historic win in the finals, the Jayappans were highly elated and Ayushman was overjoyed as he credited his win to Anamika. She had placed her confidence in him and that helped to create a healthy atmosphere. She had made him feel that he was not alone. Now things were happening which were helping them to strengthen the bond between them. However, Ayushman was still on the same mode—'no place for love' and his time was for his studies only. Anamika was scared of saying anything as she was waiting for the day when she could speak her heart out.

While all this was going on, the examination time drew near. The Board exams were to begin for students of Class X as they would now be promoted to Class XI and called seniors and for Class XII, who were now going to leave Scindia on completion of their Boards exam. They both had the same aim though their emotions were different. Ayushman got down to studying hard for his approaching exams as he had to fare well in his papers. He tried helping out Anamika too in her studies as she was not as good as he was.

It is said that Class X Boards act as a base for students as the results help them to choose whether science or humanities. And memories of Class XII exams always remain with everyone until they last. However, the results of both the classes convey what each one is cut out for. Every student could be seen with his nose immersed in some book or other. As Ayushman was exceptionally good in studies, he was given the excuse to be absent from class. He was advised to do self-studies, which gave him the opportunity to study for himself and teach others too, including Anamika. At the same time it is not enough to get good marks in Scindia School; one has to be a good all-rounder for his house. Here the housemaster had to keep a strong vigil over his house boys to ensure none played truant but studied. Marks scored in the Board exams were marks given to the respective houses. The more they scored, the better points their houses got. And in the end, a house with the maximum toppers was given the tag—Scholars.

The school trophy describes:

What is a status of the house?

What are the working abilities of the house?

Are the boys really giving time to studies?

On what are the boys concentrating?

What is the contribution of the housemaster?

Is the housemasters/housemistresses really giving time to their house activities?

Is the housemaster/housemistress really interested in knowing what his/her house is up to?

Are they exercising enough discipline to help students to grow more?

This trophy simply reflects the grandeur of the house and if some houses didn't do well, it could lead to the demotion of all the official authorities of that particular house. So it was a must to maintain a daily report of every student and it was amply clear that Ayushman would bring more laurels to his house by his all-round display. "If Ayushman does well in the Boards, then what is the harm in coming second after his house?" mumbled the housemasters till the CBSE Board results were declared.

Everyone was aware that it was no mean task to give him a fight. All tried to keep an eye on what all he studied and tried to do in the hope of achieving equally good results as he. They had one aim and that was to expose Ayushman's weakness in any possible way. They wanted to adopt the same working style as he had. Whenever they got a chance, they tried to see the subjects he was going through and follow his study routine, his formulas and rest of the work too. Most of the students woke up and went to sleep at the same time as he did. Boys were so attracted by him that it seemed as if they only had Ayushman around in the campus.

Ayushman too had noticed the phenomenon and felt somehow humbled all the more. He was told by his teachers to write a lively letter informing them what not to do. "Hello pals and thanks for the tonnes of love from you and which reaches me every day at Scindia. It is an exceptional feeling of pride for me to be here. I know you guys love the way I work and many of you want to do what I do but if you love me, then try to do what you have been doing for years, rather than doing what I am doing. Whatever I am doing is very complicated and the way I do it, it gets more complicated. I assure you that I do have a different style of working, different authors to consult or read, different things to discuss with teachers, but I am doing as I am meant to do. Similarly, you also are meant for something else. Look within to identify what it is. I request you to do things according to your own abilities. As we are different as humans, our ways to handle things would be different from each other. It is a myth that if you do all that I do, success will touch your feet. I am engaged in a number of things; therefore, you have to start from inception if you want to reach where I have. Dudes, I always say, you only have to look inside; do not adopt my style which urges individuals to go beyond, rather than live in a stable state. I do whatever my instincts tell me to do. I expect you to do your work as per your abilities," wrote Ayushman in a letter that was pasted on the notice-board. His letters helped the students to do what they were supposed to do—their own studies.

Humans take over Cigarettes

* * * * *

He was in the senior section but it seemed as if he had already established his kingdom there. He had everything running according to his own style and he was still the SR. He was captain of the junior section and had a very good equation with his seniors. Everything about him had left an indelible impact on them. He was enjoying every day, giving all possible help to others, studying what others could only imagine and raising his friends whose cause needed to be espoused. He became so illustrious that his schoolmates would stamp his footprints so that they too could gather some of the knowledge lying beneath his feet. One day, all of a sudden, this wise person was asked to give another test which he had not given so far. That day he was the only person left in his hostel as the rest were in school, attending a function. He was invariably granted permission to stay back if he so wanted so that he could do whatever was needed to study more. Sometimes, scientists need to be secluded from the rest of the world because that gives them the opportunity to experiment in peace and seclusion. However, that day what happened caught Ayushman absolutely unaware. He was not the only person left; a few seniors were present in the other rooms. He was studying in his room when two of the seniors came to him and one of them said, "We need someone to check others. Can you do us this favour?"

"What makes you ask this, sir?" Ayushman asked, somewhat rattled at this strange request.

"We are about to drink and smoke too, but we will be in our room only," added one of them. "So we need someone who can keep a vigil if anyone enters."

Since Ayushman was small in height in front of these giants, he didn't want to enter into any argument with them. But he debated in his mind, "Should I allow them to do what is not correct? After all, it is their life and what the heck have I to do with that? Do I need to care when I am not involved in any way? I am only expected to guard them for some time. Should I allow them to destroy themselves by indulging in such an activity? In any case, they will be doing whatever they want in their own rooms. I am not big enough to get into a fight and nor am I expected to report this matter to the authorities. As it is, I had already committed one mistake by reporting about my mates on an earlier occasion. I think the juniors are only meant to do what their seniors say."

As he himself had already passed through the phase of being a senior in the junior school, he knew very well that he had to respect their wishes.

All the while, his seniors stood quietly as if awaiting his verdict. "Words speak louder than action," he thought. He had been given a place from where he could see all those who entered and left the hostel. So he decided to do as he deemed fit. After they had left, he entered their room and found everyone nearly ready to celebrate for whatever the reasons were. The reasons were unknown to Ayushman.

"You are supposed to be outside; not inside," thundered one of them at Ayushman as they badly needed someone to be outside.

Ayushman replied in a simple tone, "I know I should be out, but before you start, I just want to say something."

"We feel you will also need a beer can and a cigarette while keeping guard," remarked one of the seniors, as if enjoying his discomfiture.

"No way! How can a role model do this?" remarked one senior to another. "Isn't it, Ayushman?"

"Yes, but how would you all feel if you were to become role models?" Ayushman asked.

"How?" they asked.

"It's not a big problem. All you have to do is to listen to what I have to say."

"What is it all about?" asked the seniors.

"I'll tell you a story," replied Ayushman. "A story about four friends," he added to the four seniors seated opposite him on their beds.

They were amused for a span of time. They thought that the story would be based on them only.

"What is the topic?" they asked curiously.

"Last beer, last cigarette," he replied.

"Sounds good," they said, slightly enthused by the topic. They told him to continue and kept everything aside to listen to him attentively. They pulled their beds close together to create more space and invited Ayushman to come and settle down as he stood like a statue since he had entered the room. Ayushman told them to listen properly as they were not allowed to miss a single word. He was happy to get the chance to be a storyteller for his seniors.

Ayushman began, "Round table, round glasses, round cigarettes, round bottles and everything round. These had to be sent to the nearest hospital where four persons were breathing their last breath. This is a story about four business colleagues who got together to enjoy a dint of relief after they returned from a hectic day in their respective companies in the evening. The four different friends had a lot of different things—their bank accounts, their mail ids, their girlfriends, their siblings and their tastes but in the end, they all slept together. Their lives came to an end within the clutches of their common enemy—death. That evening they brought their beer cans, wine bottles and, cigarette packets to celebrate as they had a holiday a day after. Apparently, they forgot that there are better ways of celebrating. They all took to their chairs and started boozing and smoking—a half-filled round glass in one hand and a cigarette in the other. The glasses looked very alluring when alcohol was poured into them and the cigarettes looked awesome the way they were kept on the table. They were savouring and enjoying both the things as there was no one else in the room who could get affected.

Discussing whatever they wished and recalling where they had gone wrong in their lives, they shared every misery and pain slowly. Gradually they forgot to set the limit and went on consuming one after another. Beer cans were emptied, while the wine was left untouched. Wine was brought, as they were hardcore drinkers, they would need something in the morning to get over the hangover. As luck would have it, the beer only ended their lives as they could not withstand whatever they had guzzled. They had emptied 25 cans and consumed 100 cigarettes and all of these in one single night."

"Their parents might have harboured some dreams for their sons, but in such an inebriated state, their sons had forgotten their parents and everything else they may have promised to them. Boozing combined with smoking had become a lethal poison and they divulged their lives to each other. Nearly 15 more cans and 65 cigarettes were left to be consumed and time was slipping past. They decided to talk about their future now as their past had already been discussed."

"I don't know why drunkards think that they can do whatever they want if they have a glass in their hands! I feel all this leads to severe depression thereafter. In their drunken state, they were telling each other what all they would do if they could earn large amounts of money, forgetting that a drunkard only shatters his future instead of shaping it. The after-effect of alcohol was making their heads heavy and they were finding it difficult to breathe as smoke engulfed them in the room. They were going out of their senses as they were heavily drunk by now. Five cans and 15 cigarettes were still left untouched. They still had the sense to complete the remaining stuff, though they had not the sense to think straight. Drunkards are sensible about their drinks but feel tormented when it comes to work. Gradually their appearance changed and with their lips moving and eyes looking beady, they began to rant about immaterial things. With every passing minute, they consumed more and more poison, placing their lives in jeopardy."

"Now with one can and one cigarette pack left, they had no strength left to do anything. They couldn't even wobble from one place to another, weren't able to see, weren't able to utter words coherently. They were almost close to their end. They looked almost brain-sick by now. They lay on the table for no earthly reason. They were begging for mercy. They were sorry for what they had done, but they had no one around to hear them. After a while, their smiling faces were smeared with streaming tears pouring down their cheeks. This, however, didn't deter them from taking their last sip too. All of them were looking at the central point where the can and cigarettes lay and asking themselves as to who would be the first and the last to take them. They stood up, trying to step forward, but the next moment were seen pushing each other, falling over each other, and before they could reach their destination, they were flat on the floor. Beer and cigarettes lay at the same place, that is, at the centre of the table. It is not for ITC to stop them; it is for us to fathom what it means to drink and smoke when we have no control over them."

"All the four seniors were sent to the hospital where they were declared dead and the boy who took them there was sent back with broken hopes. It was I who had taken them to the hospital. Had I stopped them, all four of them could have been working together again, but they didn't give me the opportunity to do so. I felt disheartened and crestfallen as I was in that room as the fifth person but sat there as an observer as they had their last fun of their lives."

"I had witnessed everything. I had seen them lose their senses; seen how their eyes were rolled up when they were putting their glasses to their lips; seen how their legs were wobbling as if detached from the rest of their body; and how their body and soul had got alienated in the last moments."

"When I returned to my room, I found that everything had changed except for the last beer and last cigarettes. Both were still there on the same table without having been sipped and without being fagged."

"I killed them without even touching them. Listen dudes, we don't always kill others with the help of metal equipment or by some plan. Sometimes we kill people by allowing them to do wrong things in front of us and we simply watch them because we don't want to take on the burden of anything. The same is happening right now. You are four and I am one. If you stop yourself, then we will win but if you don't stop, then I will be held responsible for killing the four of you again as I had already killed four before," concluded Ayushman.

After a short silence, he continued, "So guys, cheer up. Why are you so silent? What has happened to you all?" he asked, seeing them sitting speechless. "Could they have understood what I had meant to convey?" he asked himself. "On looking at them, it seems to have impressed them," he added to himself.

"Okay dudes, does it make any sense to you all?" he asked them, as he was keen to know what was going on in their minds.

"Such things do happen and humans do die," they all answered unanimously. The lesson had been learnt even though they may have appeared very casual about it. "We have understood these things can never be stopped, but they can be prevented from killing us. We realise that we can live long if we stop ourselves from taking them." They seemed to look guilty. There are times when we are unable to see things for ourselves and somebody has to point them out to us. At times we have to look within ourselves to discover our faults.

"Thanks for guiding us and keeping us unscathed," said the seniors to Ayushman. They were happy at this new lease of life they were given and which was far from drinks and cigarettes. And to show that they meant what they had said, they threw out all the cigarettes and cans. When they came back after disposing everything, they found a person standing and who staring at them.

"Where are you guys coming from?" he asked. He was their housemaster of Jayappa house. His expression looked ugly and his eyebrows were knit together in a frown as he could smell alcohol in their room. He told them to open their mouths and undergo the alcohol test immediately. He asked them to reach downstairs and called the doctors from the sick-room to check them. They were prepared to give any test without protesting. Ayushman stood like a spectator, as if he had no role in it all. The doctors passed them with a clear note as if they had been pregnant before and now had undergone an abortion. The housemaster had to go away empty handed as he could not see any sign of the mischief done.

They thanked Ayushman again and again. If he hadn't intervened, they would have been paying a heavy price for it all. The housemaster was relieved that there was nothing amiss while Ayushman was happy because 'words speak louder than action.' He was however a disturbed and unsatisfied soul because he had many things on his mind. He may have helped his seniors from getting into trouble, but now he had to think about the stuff lying miles away from the house.

"Why, what is the need for worrying?" asked his seniors, on finding him look worried.

"It is still unpacked, sir. So, it can be used by anyone else," said Ayushman. "Why didn't you dispose it all off properly?" he asked. "I don't want anyone to find the stuff until it has decayed. I only hope that microorganisms will work fast enough to degrade all the cans and packets. But the weather will also play a significant role in destroying the stuff."

He slowly dozed off to sleep.

Next morning, he woke up early due to the previous night's incident. In fact he had dreamt of all kinds of misgivings and had got up from the bed feeling heavy in the head. He wore his slippers, took his clothes out, served himself a Nescafe cup, went downstairs and saw an unexpected sight. A large number of water droplets lay in front of him in the cold atmosphere. It was so chilly that he felt as if he was inside a refrigerator. He saw damp sand at the corners and fields which by now were filled with water. He enjoyed the sight and all of a sudden he saw a drop fall into his cup as if it was the last one remaining. Then he realised that it had rained last night and therefore he had felt the same in his dreams too. He looked up at the sky and said, "Thank for giving me one last blessing. In fact, I am very happy to be given what I had hoped for last night—bad weather.

Tension of Boards, 2003

* * * * *

Board exams began on March 1, 2003 and everyone could be seen burning the midnight oil to be able to fare well in the exams. It was essential to pass in every paper they were giving. Each of them was trying to put in his very best so as to be ahead of the nearest rival. In school, rivalry is at its peak, be it against a friend or an adversary.

Ayushman could be seen with a book in his hand at all times and seemed ever more conscientious than before. Be it a talk about any house, the student were seen trying to put in his best. In fact, the CBSE Boards are all about those who dare to confront any problem in their life, who know how to take the bull by the horns and how to deal with both easy and difficult question papers with equal felicity. The Scindians were not only taught to score good marks, but how to deal with papers through proper time management. They had to bring into play every kind of game plan they had in their mind and attack the paper with full ferocity. As the Board dates had been declared, the students looked like bookworms prowling in every corner of the school building.

"However, let every house adopt the best game plan, though in the end it is an adroit house which will win the trophy by scoring the highest marks. After all, it is a question of the Scholar Trophy," whispered the teachers among themselves. Everyone had lots of expectations from Ayushman as if he way the only brilliant boy at Scindia School. Scindia hosts the Board examinations as it is best at organising them. It is the place where everyone reaches to give his/her examination for Class X or XII Board exam, no matter from which school he or she is.

"Perhaps we can cheat," thought every boy in school as they had invigilators from their own school; they had their own people who served as supervisors.

"At least I can hide in my pockets some chits, as it is my school."

"At least I can write something on my collars, as it is my own school."

"I don't need to study that hard as I am giving my papers in my own school with my own teachers."

"Perhaps not, as it is not someone's private property. It is Scindia School," said the teachers, concerned as they were about protecting the image of their own school.

Everyone prepared to do exceptionally well in their examinations, but an unexpected fear choked their throats somewhere. It was not only a tough time for those who were giving the papers, but even for all the housemasters. They had to attend thousands of calls from the parents of children preparing for the Boards. Calls were made even to their residences to verify their children's report cards and housemasters had to answer all the questions/queries, no matter what time they received the calls.

March 2003. The Boards began. The subjects were English, Mathematics, Hindi, Social Sciences and Pure Sciences.

Students felt, while giving their Boards, that they were stationed somewhere on the border, fighting for their country. But for Ayushman it was a challenge and a pleasant one at that time as it helped him to gauge his understanding of the subject. Along with the technical examination, the boys were found awake till late at night, lying somewhere in corners, mumbling phrases, memorising the concepts, asking for the leftovers and praying a lot. However, Ayushman was found calm and cool as a cucumber. He didn't believe in taking any tension for any of his examination. He would wake up by 8 or 8.50 a.m., tell others a few things which they might not have understood the previous night due to over-complexities, give time in getting dressed himself as it was important to breathe easy, come out in the balcony to see the sunrise and build up a lot of energy to be able to fight the exam monster. Finally he would walk slowly to the examination hall where he would be the only person to ask for the question paper and always the first to submit his answer sheets without a moment's delay. No one was as quick as he was. He didn't feel any need at any point of time to recheck his papers. Come to think of it, Ayushman himself was an answer sheet for all his Scindian schoolmates and no one could ever prove him wrong. Acting as a soothsayer, he would often placate his friends and tell them what questions could possibly be expected. Boys would approach him whenever they saw him coming out of the examination hall. He had no time to see his own paper and check how well he could have done. But he had to listen to the problems among others. Ayushman was so good with his calculations, formulae, numerical ability that he would sit anywhere to hear their problems and solve their queries. Teachers tried to help as best as they could, but they never failed to notice Ayushman helping out the students as if he were the principal himself. They always knew that this would happen and therefore they respected Ayushman for all his help. The Boards are never easy for anyone. Ayushman had noticed some of his friends crying as they feared they might flunk, while some others were seen indulging in light-hearted revelry on performing well in their Boards. Some enjoyed giving examinations and some became so tense that they had to swallow pills to soothe their agitated nerves.

As it was too late to do anything now, and realisation at this last moment was of no use.

As soon as the exams got over, the students become excited to return to their respective homes and enjoy a long summer holiday of about four months or so. One's home is always an ideal place to relax and forget about examinations and results.

Before departing from school, every student meets the other, promising to stay in touch through the phone or the post. Some are happy to leave, while some are sad and a few are in an in-between state of happiness and sorrow.

They all know that during their vacations they have to wait for their results to be declared and plan what to do next. Everyone had to wait, watch and see—Ayushman at his home, Anamika at hers and the teachers of Scindia at the fort. Some even wanted the CBSE results to be announced the next day itself as the wait for the results could absolutely kill anyone. Much was expected of Ayushman as he was the most deserving candidate in the school and who had every chance of winning the school trophy. However, Ayushman's mind was far from such thoughts. He was as calm as ever, exam or no exam. He neither felt proud of anything he did and neither seemed complacent at his success. He maintained an even keel.

The silence broke when the results were finally declared. Who could stop the CBSE from announcing their results? They are a much respected Board in the nation for their fair and just play.

The endless hours of waiting came to an end as the results were out on the internet, mobile, television and newspapers. Every mobile company had a unique way to announce the results as if they were the kingmakers. These facilities were open to all those who were interested in knowing their results while staying at home only. They were free to choose any mode—either by sitting next to their parents or in their sealed rooms. While some students ran here and there, making their way through the crowd to learn what their destiny held in store for them, Ayushman slowly walked out to find out the results himself.

He was more concerned about knowing how his friends had fared and was less interested in learning about his own results. Most students could be seen chaperoned by their parents, while a few came with their girlfriends/ friends, and still fewer were alone too.

"Different attitudes can always be seen in students every year, no matter which results are declared," thought Ayushman. He was all alone and keenly observing everything while heading towards the nearest café. He noticed that many parents had tied red or black threads around their son's or daughter's neck or wrist as if this could prove lucky for their offspring. Some of them had a red *tilak* on their forehead and others had some item placed in their right pockets which would ensure their success. In fact, some students sat at home with the priest or an astrologer, hoping that this would help them to fare well in the examination. Good, maybe their priest knew more than the Microsoft engineers, or maybe their priest could perform some miracle to help their marks increase. Ayushman wondered if Bill Gates also had some priest next to him when he inaugurated his company, the Microsoft.

"Is it good to be so spiritual rather than materialistic?" asked Ayushman of himself and replied, "Do I really need to worry about things as the other does when concerned with the results?" He moved at a fast pace towards the notice-board.

Soon his destination appeared in front of him. He felt elated to see the building as his marks would non be in front of his eyes. He entered the building through the main gate which had twelve floors. The internet facility was available on the third floor. It was the place where the fate of many students was going to be decided.

There was a lot of rush due to the CBSE results. The café was up in the building, for which a few steps had to be climbed. As it was the city's most renowned cyber-café, most inhabitants used to gather here. The building seemed unpleasant to him as he witnessed some happy but more withdrawn faces on the steps. It was the time when no one was aware of the other as the focus of each was on one thing only—the results. He was about to skip up the staircase, when his eyes fell on a student coming downstairs, tears pouring down his cheeks.

"What a start I just had!" remarked Ayushman. "I am also human, dude. Every topper too suffers from anxiety," he added. He went up and as he completed the first round of the staircase, he found another boy crying in one corner. He became more anxious and petrified this time. He couldn't decide what to do. He felt impeded, as if his legs had got detached and were telling him not to go up.

As he completed another round of the staircase, he found a family slapping their child due to the marks he had scored. He found himself feeling more and more depressed and downhearted after seeing such sights. He said to himself only one more round to go, though all the macabre scenes had robbed him of his interest in the results. His face looked pale with a mixed expression of fear and suspense. He was devoid of the spirit which he had felt on starting from his room. Finally he completed the last round of the staircase and reached the café. He sat down in front of a computer but all kinds of gory pictures kept coming in his mind. He began to feel somewhat woozy and wasn't able to sense anything. A chill ran down his spine and he lost control over his body. He slowly recovered to his senses and began to log in. He opened 'Google' and found the CBSE results online. The computer showed a square on the screen asking for his name and roll number to be entered. Ayushman filled his name and before he could fill the next, another bad news arrived when he heard someone announce that a boy had jumped off the building. It was a twelve-storey building Now, he felt totally hopeless and ran back to his room without bothering to find out his result.

As the results were out, a number of students waited outside his room to find out his results, but what they saw in front made them wonder what had gone amiss for they had never seen him in a condition like this ever before. His eyes were red, his body shivered and he suffered from fluctuating body temperature.

At Anamika's request, he recounted all his experiences from A to Z while she consoled him over the telephone. As he had no energy left to see further, he kept himself confined to his room. Two days later, he received the results by ordinary post from his school. That day he received two pieces of news—one about his marks and the other about the five students who had died out of the twenty-five by commiting suicide due to their bad results in the examination.

He was utterly confused as he did not know whether to rejoice or weep. He went through his report card and read, 'Abilities like no one has.' He had comfortably topped his whole batch of Class X. His knowledge, concepts, arguments, analyses led everyone to bow in front of him—his clear diagrammatical representations in sciences, long written paragraphs in social sciences, language clearance in Hindi, equation solving in mathematics, vocabulary in English and ability in all subjects. Not only had he impressed his school authorities but the examiners of the CBSE too. He was the only one in CBSE to score more than 95 in six subjects, out of which he scored above 98 in three, 99 in two and 100 in one. But Ayushman's family couldn't enjoy their happiness as the results had arrived a bit too late when their excitement had somewhat waned.

Mediapersons flocked to his residence to interview him. But the interview didn't go well, as one of the journalists began by saying, "Would you be able to enjoy your results at a time when five students around you have committed suicide?"

All he could do was to reply lamely, "What others do is their own perception; I am not responsible for their irresponsible behaviour. But out of humanity, I will not celebrate my success publicly." Ayushman abruptly called off the interview as he felt terribly pissed off with them.

Ayushman had prepared a long list of guests and this meant distribution of over a thousand cards but everything was cancelled at the last moment. Anamika too had fared well but her marks were not that impressive as his.

"Why didn't you beat me in the results?" asked Ayushman of her.

"Teachers always remain at the top, sir," she said.

"I just wanted your presence during my preparations which I had comfortably," she thought. "Who cares about results when love has already taken over?"

Anamika and Ayushman were in their respective cities at the time of the CBSE results. They couldn't meet each other as Ayushman had left for the vacations soon after giving his papers. They decided to share their success with each other by being at one place. He invited Anamika for the celebration and she turned up at his home. She was excited to visit his home as she felt that one day she would be doing this only, then why not do it now? Ayushman didn't have to devote much time in persuading her to come when he asked her come over.

He felt grateful to have Anamika at his house. He introduced her to his family members. Anamika stayed behind to spend a couple of days with his family before returning back to school.

Dint of Seniority

* * * * *

Ayushman returned to Gwalior with Anamika. It was the August of 2003.

"I wish this year could do more for you," said Anamika to him, on the way.

"With his talent, Ayushman needs to join the only science stream to get more honed," felt the science block.

"When he is so good in the sciences, we cannot estimate his worth if he comes in commerce. So send him to us," said the commerce block.

"Let him choose whatever he wants," said the principal.

And in the end, he chose the most expected, essential, indispensable path for him to learn more—the sciences. Many of his friends couldn't get the science stream as they didn't fulfil the basic requirements. They had to opt for the commerce stream, but they weren't disappointed because for them what was important was to study in Scindia School. They could have been sent back home had their results not been up to the mark.

Ayushman chose the sciences to get more from life. His friends had to get into the sciences as they were told by their parents to do so and Anamika had to be in the sciences so that she could see more of Ayushman—be near him, hear him and propose to him one day. Unluckily she got commerce as she couldn't fulfil the basic requirement. She had hoped to get a minimum of 65 per cent in mathematics, but she could score only 62 per cent. If only she could have got 3 per cent more, she would have been in the science stream with Ayushman.

Both of them were promoted to Class XI. Needless to say, Ayushman now got the chance to run his house in a proper manner. Only Classes XI and XII could run their respective houses, apart from the hostel authorities and the housemasters/housemistresses. And when Class XII drew nearer to their Boards, then the baton of command was handed over to somebody from Class XI. As it is not possible for a Class XII students to devote all their time for development of the house, it becomes necessary to hand over the duties of the house to someone who can lead it to victory and success. There is even a tiny demarcation to show this subtle difference between the seniors and juniors where the latter have to wear shorts, while the seniors are allowed to wear trousers. This only meant that if anyone was caught cooking something crooked around the campus, any trouser among the many could emerge as a potent monitor to teach him a lesson, be it verbal or physical.

Ayushman was the only guy at Scindia who had enjoyed every bit of seniority in his early classes because of his meticulous behaviour and finesse. The powers vested him in the early years were enough for his batchmates to vent anger upon him. He never felt like a junior when he was a junior himself. In fact, he always kept the most malleable attitude towards his seniors and therefore was never assailed by anyone. He neither was told to do any work for anyone nor was he disturbed while doing his own. Therefore, he always managed to study and find time to devote to Anamika. However, differences were there between them but they managed to brush them aside. As he was the most diligent soul in school, he was least beaten up and least ragged till he became a senior himself. In fact, many a time he helped his seniors in their subjects. He had simply relished all his junior classes while doing his own work.

Now he was not in the mood to recall what all he had done in his previous classes. He had to be best again and had to show that even a bookworm could encourage his housemates properly. His seniority placed many more responsibilities upon him and he knew more were yet to come in the near future. The prefects of Scindia School enjoy substantial powers but the below-mentioned positions can only be given to Class XII students.

House prefect is a local representative of a house having nothing to do at school level but to act on behalf of his house only.

School prefect singularly represents his house at school level. He often represents his house wherever he goes or vice-versa, but he has limited powers. He has nothing to do with other houses. He can only make some suggestions and it is not essential for the others to follow. Giving commands in any case is not allowed unless the school prefect of the other house comes up for negotiations.

School captain is a position which demands a potent will, a sharp mind, an adroit workstyle and a tough body. This supreme power always goes to a boy who has the potential to differentiate himself from others. He can easily rule over any prefect, any house and any boy that he wants. He can always state his opinion in any matter he wishes. The entire school dances to his tune. The relation between the captain and the school is closely interlinked. The school expects the captain to be a role model and the captain wants the school to give him his space. But this unrivalled power given to the captain was yet to come in his life. Appointing Ayushman as a school captain was like a dream for everyone at Scindia. They eagerly waited for Ayushman to become the captain as if he was the only guy to go to the moon. Ayushman was excited when told in the junior school that he could be the captain again on reaching Class XII. But for now he was satisfied to be with what he was—a Class XI student who had been given seniority.

He was a second-class senior and so was Anamika. She had lived in her parental home as though she was a Barbie doll. So, for her to be a senior was not negotiable. She had no companion except her Mom; she had no one to rule over except her Mom; and she had no one to wipe her tears whenever she cried over Ayushman other than her Mom. The moment he became senior, new rules were enforced in his house for better functioning. It seemed as if he was trying to curb all acts, good or bad, which had happened when the house was run by one of his seniors. He planned and tried to give a new shape to his Jayappa house.

What is more, whatever he did, the rest followed, participating eagerly in all the activities. Everyone obeyed him and no one was bold enough to say 'no' to him. The reasons for this are no longer unknown to anyone. Above all, there was no harm in saying 'yes' to Ayushman because whatever he did, he did it for the welfare of the house only. He wanted to introduce a new life among the Jayappans by assigning them special tasks. As he had been a junior himself some time ago, he knew very well what a tiny spark could do in one's life. He had some plans for his juniors to ignite their lives as if he wanted to redress everyone.

"I want you to keep doing the things for the house. Do whatever you think you are best at. Put your hand in everything so that you could know what you are meant for and it will be beneficial for you and for the house as well. See, as long as you are here at Scindia, you have the time to experiment, to know what actually you are. Listen, it is not necessary for every Scindian to join the IIT, Amity, IcfaiTech, BITS Pilani, Anna University, Punjab Engineering College, Vellore Institute of Technology, JNTU, SRM, Motilal Nehru National Institute of Technology, Dhirubhai Ambani, IIC or others for graduation. Some of you can even go for sports, writing, politics, Indian defence forces, films and more, but you have to find what comes first in your life. What are your priorities? And if you want to study only, then do it but no one from this house should be seen studying always. You have to contribute in sports as well because it helps a person to stay physically fit. And it improves the stamina too. If someone is not good in a particular thing, then there are other multiple options. If you are not good in cricket, then go in for hockey, or basketball, or football and so on until you know what you are good at. If you are unable to perform on the field, doesn't matter. You can always go in for track events like athletics, cross-country races and more. If you are a failure in both, then become a speaker and start speaking on the stage by participating in elocutions, debates as it kills the inner fear of pubic speaking. And if you show yourself useless to me in every field, then I will make you to perform in everything until you have no breath left," said Ayushman to all his fellow-mates just to motivate them. He knew he had the power to revamp and refurbish his house now.

This speech conveyed a clear message to everyone that they had to work for the house and gradually they had to 'live for the house'. This became the anthem of the Jayappans too.

At the same time he never neglected his studies and showed his positive aspect in everything. He joined the science group but unluckily, Anamika had to join the commerce group. Poor darling, he thought! It was not anyone's fault; it was sheer destiny which had decided their fate and of everyone precisely. Thus, they were both in different streams. When he was in Class XI, he showed his interest in almost every activity and won numerous awards. His contribution in school activities had proved encouraging for many others of the school as they wanted to emulate him.

His desire was not only to be the hero at Scindia School; he wanted to be an exceptional in all that he did through the dint of hard work. Did he really become so? Let's read more.

He was apt to giving lectures in different sections when he was in Class XI as no one else was as capable as he was. And no teacher said anything to him as they had the fear of demotion in their minds. He used to teach his schoolmates how to strive for technology and how to use it for the right purposes. But somewhere, somehow, sometimes he always felt someone's absence in his life. It could have been anything—status, success, ambition, love, family. During his journey through Class XI, he was asked to submit the best entry in the science stream of the school. He was given the 'Best Entry' award too in 2003, when he had just entered the seniority zone.

Meanwhile Anamika missed him a lot as they were not only in different sections, his popularity left him with no to go anywhere or meet anyone else at the fort except a few local authorities. "I wonder where I am and where my heart is," wondered Anamika, whenever she found herself alone. Many a time she felt as though there was no one in this world for her.

Her mother knew every thing as Anamika had told her all just as most girls do. It is somehow difficult for a girl not to divulge her secrets to another female. "I should have stopped myself before but I didn't, so there is no point in regretting. It is too difficult for me to forget him as I am madly in love with him," Anamika told her Mom, placing her head on the latter's lap.

Months passed and everytime the sun arose, she resolved to do more to prove her love. She had not left a single place at the fort where she didn't go to escape from the memories of her love. If it had been so easy to forget everything, then there would have been no cases of suicide which lovers resort to when madly in love. She found herself in a horrific situation as not only were they in different sections, but leading different lives too. If she could confide in someone as she used to in him, if she could see someone with whom she bonded as she did with him, and if she could eat something and feel as though he was feeding her, her life would have become so simple. No matter what she did, it all brought back memories of the time spent with him. Even her sleep brought him in her dreams. Lovers often take sleeping pills to sleep quickly and deeply, but she kept herself awake for months so that nothing related to him would escape.

Ayushman was miles away from her. She had nothing but his memories to live upon and survive. She felt deeply depressed while Ayushman continued earning accolades in whatever he did. He became a regular winner and his name was announced frequently in the assembly hall. He was called on to the stage every now and then. He won awards for writing science fiction, for writing essays describing the importance of technology, for helping the department in metal work, woodwork, paperwork, photography and in helping the school to create an eco-friendly environment for students at the fort. It became a routine for teachers as also the principal to hear words lauding him almost every morning.

He could completely set the stage on fire when asked to speak. It took another decade for others to see someone else receive such adulation on the stage. Couldn't anyone stand in front of him? Perhaps no and what is more, he often had to compete with himself only. He received so many certificates that he had to order a separate cupboard to store them. Sometimes he had to send a courier home to reduce the number of certificates and create space for other things.

It so happened that his name had become synonymous with the morning prayers. Apparently, Anamika was left as a part of the crowd to watch from afar. He had practically stopped talking, though it was unwittingly done. She had become serious due to his absence, but was somewhat glad at his successes. Ayushman's indifferent attitude only helped her to face the uneven tenor of her life. Meanwhile, Ayushman understood that without success, a person is like an empty barrel. So it was better for everyone to engage in some work to lead a purposeful life.

"When you do things well, you have to keep doing things well all the time," he told his friends once and everyone understood the significance of his words and why he could spare no time for anyone. "Success is not your friend. Your fame requires lesser time to get corrupted than it does to earn. So always do well to avoid letting it get spoilt." He also had words of encouragement for his friends when they did well. He never refrained from saying a few words in the morning to boost the morale of others. The sun wakes up life on this planet, while Ayushman served to wake up students from their stupor and strive hard to do well. His words worked like a tonic for many students.

Ayushman exercised quite some influence, but he did not use it on anyone with the purpose of hurting him. He never showed boorish behaviour towards any junior and maintained an ambience of well-being all around him. He took up projects with his housemasters and signed for other ventures with outsiders. His speed in completing his projects was remarkable. Once he took up eight different projects underneath four different teachers. No one was ever allowed at Scindia to take on so many projects as the CBSE did not permit it either. So his teachers made it clear that whatever he scored on his projects would not be included in the final marksheet for Class XII, except for two only and here he was given the choice to include whatever he desired.

"I have not taken up all this extra work to score marks only. I took these up to learn something more than required by the school or the Board. Scoring marks is not my only objective," he would clarify to all and sundry.

His work earned appreciation and was duly applauded in the assembly. There were some students who out of jealousy indulged in backbiting. Whenever he did something laudatory, some of them waited to see what was so important about his task.

They could be seen whispering, "What work does he have?"

The teachers would ask each other, "Will this work prove fruitful in the end? What if his work earns disrepute? Will he really make it big? Is he interested in becoming some kind of a genius like Bill Gates? Is he keen to join an MNC? Does he desire to own a White House in his name?" All these questions had become a part of their normal conversation, though all these queries went futile as Ayushman refuted all such claims. His argument was, "I am just trying to become someone and whatever I am doing right now has to be done like this only. I will tell you all about it when the time is ripe for it."

He was so keen to learn more that every day he got himself involved in something new to solve. Loads of work mounted on his head and time seemed to be running out. However, not to be deterred, he was ready to face any eventuality. Whenever he found himself losing heart or becoming lax in his work, he would cajole his body to put in more effort and work with renewed vigour. He made himself incommunicado for the next few months so that he could devote utmost concentration on his projects. The reason for it could be any, but the main one was that a boy like him could not be expected to give away his spare time over insignificant activities. His curiosity and keenness to learn more by participating in meetings based on his projects served to feed his hungry mind, which wanted to absorb more and more. He was drawing near to becoming a scientist.

While most students study as they have been forced to do so or merely to pass the exams, Ayushman knew exactly how to make his studies interesting. He devoured every possible book, deciphered every possible theme, demystified the unknown and became the only person in the school to explain the why and how of every concept and derivation. Somehow he was in full control of his mind. He could instruct his body, soul and mind to do whatever he wanted. He knew clearly what he wanted and therefore worked towards achieving it. In his endeavour to succeed, he put all his friendships and relations on hold. As a consequence, Anamika was made to suffer more than what she could bear. It seemed as if he had gone underground for a while.

Desires Unplugged

*****

Ayushman was engaged in completing his projects. He ensured that his theory work ran parallel to his practical. He had no other desire except to expedite whatever was on hand. His determination did not allow him to wander far from his teachers and his pleasant nature kept him close to his teachers.

By now Anamika had begun to lose everything that she could. Firstly, Ayushman didn't talk to her as he was busy with his huge work load; secondly, as a result, she could not concentrate on her studies; thirdly, again as a result, she was given to frequent bouts of depression. If Ayushman were only to talk to her, she could have hoped for something, but in the current situation, all seemed to have been lost. She began to visit the science block where Ayushman used to study. This prompted his teachers to admonish them as it hindered and diverted his concentration. But her heart refused to listen. All she wanted was to meet him and exchange a few words with him. But her brazen behaviour only earned for both of them insults and embarrassment. She was banned from entering the science block without seeking prior permission. Normally commerce students are not allowed to enter the science block during school hours as everyone knows that science students need to concentrate and devote more time to experiments and projects. So Anamika became the first one in the whole school to be banned from going there. Teachers had no alternative but to stop her strictly. Ayushman felt no difference as he did not have time to delve into such things. Some felt that both Ayushman and Anamika were right while others considered it was Anamika's fault to disturb the boy's concentration and still a few felt that both were doing what they loved most.

In any case, Ayushman, in his desire to be the best among all, pushed everything and everyone on the backburner. Anamika was in love, so she had to be with him. But like her heart, her tottering steps weren't able to improve their relationship. Ayushman was not free and had become more reticent than ever before. She didn't know what she could do—"Should I interrupt his work by forcing him to pay attention to me or should I help him as a good friend?" she debated in her mind.

"Do you find love difficult to handle, darling?" asked Anamika's mother one day, in an effort to console her in some way.

"I know I am disturbing him a lot, but what can I do, Mom? My intensions are not to leave him to himself. I want him to be close by my side. When I don't find all these things, then I go insane. I strive to bolster his spirits whenever I see them sag, don't I? But nothing is helping me to accomplish my aim. I feel as though he is going far from me and I am unable to find any solution to it. I have loved him since the day my eyes fell on him, but tell me, Mom, why isn't our relationship working right? Whenever I see him, all my resolutions go flying out of the window. What to do now? Should I wait for a no-ball sign? Listen Mom, I have only one aim and that is to possess him. I will keep loving him till he is mine and if things don't go well, I will die," she concluded lamely to her Mom.

Her mother replied sadly, "I think I have produced a completely blind person who can't make out what the other feels about her. Maybe scientists need to be secluded only, dear." She tried to console her daughter as best as she could but the daughter had become so crazy in love that she used to escape from her classes to catch a glimpse of him anywhere around the campus. Whenever his friends would see her, they would ask her jocularly, "What's cooking?" She would smile weakly at them as she herself did not know what was happening. She tried her best to draw Ayushman away from his work, but he seemed unaware of her presence and all he knew was to move with the flow.

Generally, Arjun sir and Ayushman worked together on his projects in the school labs. Everything had been moving smoothly when a slight problem arose. Both of them were winding up their work and getting ready to return to their rooms when all of a sudden the unexpected happened. As they had been inside the lab for long, both came out to take a breath of fresh air. They decided to take a walk together to rejuvenate themselves. Both were absolutely fagged out and so engrossed in their work that they felt the need for fresh air. And, like any other scientist, Arjun sir decided to invite Anamika to join them on their walk. He rang her up at her mother's residence to say, "Come as soon as possible outside the science block. We both are taking a walk. Join us if you can." This he did when Ayushman's attention was caught elsewhere. He did not want to reveal his plan to Ayushman.

When they had taken a few steps ahead, Anamika arrived and joined them for the walk. Even P.T. Usha couldn't have run as fast as she had done to reach them. She was with them in a jiffy as if she had been waiting for someone to tell her to run.

"Hi," greeted Ayushman, though terribly fatigued and after inhaling a long breath. He was nonetheless surprised to see her there and took a minute or so to get over the shock.

"Hi! It seems we are meeting after a long hiatus," she replied joyfully.

"I could have met you often if only you had not been banned from coming here," he said. "Perhaps, we had met a day earlier only."

"Yes, how can I forget? I was crossing the street and you waved through your window. You didn't even feel it necessary to come out, Ayushman. Will you call that mere wave of recognition as having met?" she asked complainingly.

"Sorry, I was busy at that time."

"You have been busy for years, Ayushman."

"But today you have come here at the right time," he said.

"Why, what happened?" she asked him.

"Today I would like to tell you about my most ardent desire," Ayushman said to both of them.

"What is it?"

"It can be anything. Just have patience," he replied and then he asked her and Arjun sir to walk ahead.

While this exchange was going on, Arjun sir hadn't deemed it necessary to utter a single word. He wanted to give them time to chat with each other. He was walking with them as if he was not there.

Anamika, Arjun sir and Ayushman wandered over the lonely streets for some time as if they had no place to go to. Actually they were on the lookout for the right place to sit as by now they were tired sitting in front of air-conditioners which were fitted on every window of their classrooms and laboratories. Suddenly they all stopped near a tree so that they could breathe some fresh air. After casting suspicious glances at each other, they all sat down. The three of them sat around the tree as if the tree was the collar while they were the fussy tie wound around its neck…

"I won't get a day better than this to say 'I love you,'" Anamika thought. But by the time Anamika could open her mouth, he had already expressed his wishful thinking to them. She longed to speak out what she desired the most, but somehow couldn't. Both of them had received a good chance to speak out what was in their minds but only one of them got the opportunity to use it.

Ayushman said, "The moment I set foot inside Scindia School, I went into deep meditation till I took my second step. In the whole process, I realised that my world had changed and taken a more concrete shape and form. I even started imagining that I had become a scientist. I don't know how this happened to me. Was I the only one to get affected on seeing Scindia or were there others like me, I cannot say. I didn't find the answer and neither was I supposed to find it. It has been so long since I started my work in school that the feel of a being scientist has become more plausible with every passing day. It is not because I am completing my schooling from Scindia, but I have actually started feeling that I have a scientist in me."

"Everyone begins with small steps and gradually sets up a strong foundation to build his empire as the Tatas and Ambanis have done. Each of them harboured strong ambitions and they worked towards them and fulfilled their desires and maybe they have still more to fulfil and rise higher. My desire is to make you feel that we have to be ambitious to achieve something. They all were born inexperienced as you or me, but today they are what we are not. In fact, in their initial days, when they used to play with balls, they were not as popular as they are today. So what makes them different and successful? It comes from their way to 'feel' things. They know how to work on dreams and I have learnt by reading about them to be conscientious. In fact, I have learnt from every successful person how to be quick in work. If something has to be done, then we have to plan from A to Z, which I have been doing for years now. Secondly, we need to know how we can become more charismatic so that we can attract more people to share their innovations with us.

"Every human being is not complete in young age. We are born with all kinds of limitations which need to be overcome sooner or later. Lack of dedication is the most common drawback amongst us. Here in Scindia, ample opportunities are provided to increase our energy levels and become more ambitious. We have to feel big and recognise ourselves well. It is this factor which makes us 'Sc-Indians'. And as I had already realised this point, I started working immediately upon it. I would even like you, Anamika, to feel the same way as I have felt; maybe you would do much better than what I am doing in life—by not being a scientist, but something else that you want."

Ayushman went on and on and both his companions could not understand how such a youngster was so focused in life! When one enters a school, one is often more inclined towards indulging in naughty things, but Ayushman, the prospective scientist, had a lot to say to them. They kept silent and Ayushman continued his speech with the same vibrant zeal.

"A few decades ago, Newton was the man, who while sitting under a tree and waiting for the unexpected to happen, experienced the unexpected. An apple fell on his head. He didn't eat it; instead he began to think what could have made it fall. Thereafter he read and experimented continuously till he termed that 'fall' of the 'apple' as 'g'. He gave us the concept of gravity, which we all have been using for years now and none of us has ever realised that 'g' is a complete entity, having its own existence with the stated reasons."

"What are you trying to say, Ayushman?" interjected Arjun sir. "Are you saying that Newton has sent you on earth to tell us this thing?" he added.

"No sir," said Ayushman. "Perhaps the other person," said Ayushman, contradicting him.

"Who is he?" Arjun sir asked. "Do I know him?"

"Not only you, but the whole world knows him," replied Ayushman proudly.

Arjun sir and Ayushman stood face to face, discussing the great scientists of the time. They were recalling their names, their work, their support and love which helped in inventing something new for all of us. However, Anamika was cursing Newton to have been so great that Ayushman could see him only, remember him only, feel him in his absence but couldn't see her love which she had tried to convey in so many ways. She was as confused as Arjun sir.

"In a similar manner, there was one more eminent person who achieved the unbelievable when he discovered the Theory of Relativity. His name was Albert Einstein, who gave us $E=mc^2$. But can anyone tell me from where did the derivation come? Tell me sir, does any formula hold any importance till it is derived? We may simply state that formula sans derivation but it has no meaning until someone comes up to complete it. I hope my aim has become clear to you by now. And I am, Ayushman Agarwal, proudly working on this since I began to feel like a scientist. And I would love being Einstein-II because someone is always born to do these things. Someone is born to realise someone else's dreams," concluded Ayushman, leaving both the listeners speechless.

"I always knew that you wanted to be a scientist but do you have an idea what all you would have to forsake for realising you dream?" Arjun sir asked him.

"Everything except my life, sir," he replied, as if he knew everything.

"It might take your life even, Ayushman," said Arjun sir, deeply touched.

"Now you tell me, sir, can you suggest anything further? Can you tell me what all I may need to fulfil my dream?"

"Listen, you are good but even I don't know what to say over this issue," Arjun sir replied. "To tell you frankly, I have never found a person who wants to do this," he added. "As we are talking about $E=mc^2$, I wonder what I should say to you Ayushman. Even Anamika and Anuradha didn't tell me about this ever."

"I got to know about this Newton and Einstein stuff only today," said Anamika.

"Good, when you didn't tell them, then how could I expect anything else?"

"We are not talking about the degree of expectancy here. We are talking about something as hard core science, sir. Kindly suggest to me what should I do?"

"Okay, all is well, but what prompted you to derive this?"

"No one has come up to me with this. It is just my inner voice which prompted me," said Ayushman.

"How can someone's inner voice urge him/her to derive this formula, dear?" asked Arjun sir.

"How do I know, sir? How can I feel the opposite of what I have felt? How can I tell why I felt this? After all, it's all about a feel only," he said in order to convince Arjun sir anyhow.

"Do me a favour," Arjun sir said endearingly.

"What?" Ayushman asked.

"Tell your inner voice not to make you feel like this any more."

"Really, sir?" Ayushman asked. "Do you really think that if I start on this formula, I would be left with more time to do anything else? I mean this will take a lot of time."

"When, where, and how will you start?" asked Arjun sir as he had to take interest in him for he was like a family member besides being a student too.

"As you can see, I have already started," said Ayushman.

"Tell me one more thing, Ayushman. You have done remarkably well in your studies, taken part in every science-related work, helped students, assisted teachers, joined new ventures with other schools/teachers, undertaken many projects, taken your own stand. Has everything been done to start the same thing, Ayushman?" Arjun sir asked him very politely as if to clear his doubts.

"No sir, how can I have the pictures of such stalwarts in my mind at so early stage? Moreover, I can only say that I have been trying my best to get started. I have been doing all the stuff, not to start the same, but to achieve what I am born for. And now I have realised that what I have to do is $E=mc^2$. When I entered Scindia, I resolved that I will give cent per cent everywhere to learn what I am good at. Practicing and developing various experiments, going through every kind of book, understanding the concepts, writing theses, all these things helped me identify what I can do and what I can take up, sir."

"First you made up your mind on what you wanted to be—a scientist probably. Second, you tried to find out what it takes to be one—so a lot of hard work probably. Third, you worked on your meandering paths to know the depths —probably about the topic. Fourth and finally, you have chosen the undisputed formula, $E=mc^2$. Many degree-holders haven't been able to do it so far. Now you would try to solve/derive it with all your past experiences and without any higher degree," Arjun sir said. "What a resolution made in life, dude! I would love to see a Class XII student competing with Einstein, Ayushman," Arjun sir added.

Both of them had a long conversation, but Anamika kept quiet during the whole session. Once or twice she did try put in a word or two, but Ayushman's long description of his objective made her feel unwanted. What is more, Arjun sir couldn't do anything to help her as he was not allowed to say much either. He felt useless. He tried to give their relationship a realistic vision, but he ended up saying something else. Ayushman wanted to be the next Einstein. Arjun sir had got a new student like Einstein and Anamika was the only one who felt empty handed, tormented and forced to observe silence.

Anamika had felt like an outsider many a times because of his preoccupation with his own work or that of some other student or so. Ayushman's professional dream was acting like an obstacle in her life. "Here I had been praying for his success in the Class XII Boards exam so that once he got over them, we could spend time with each other, but now I find that it was just wishful thinking and nothing more. Now I feel I will have to increase my hours of prayer and subsequently my age will increase too. If Ayushman would keep himself involved in this kind of tedious work, I wonder what would happen in the end. If his work will continue like this, then I won't be able to get married until I become 80 or so," thought Anamika to herself, completely disheartened. "If he had been so interested in the sciences, then he should have gone to some other planet to do his research. He doesn't deserve me. Why did he come here to Scindia School to piss us off? Is it true that 'love at first sight' has certain limits? Does love at first sight mean that it is not lasting love? Does love at first sight ever get fulfilled?"

Her mother also began to think likewise on seeing her daughter's plight. She had full sympathy with her daughter and tried to console her by saying that nothing would go wrong. If you were look at it objectively, there really was nothing wrong between them. Her mother would tell her, "It is all about having patience and behave serenely until you get what you want or until your partner begins to desire the same thing as you do. This happens with everyone who falls in love. If you get what you want, then nothing like it. If not, then you cannot do anything until the partner feels the same way as you do. You need to respect his every desire and his every mood." Her mother never refrained from giving her advice and like a good daughter, Anamika tried to do as was deemed fit. She knew there was no point in going violent on him or exhibiting her emotions openly. She couldn't say anything after going through deep pain in her life and no one knew about her plight except her Mom. Moreover, she was forced to ask herself, "Who should be blamed for all this—Newton, the man who showed everyone that even an apple can help in discovering the concept of 'g', or Einstein, the man who didn't prove what he knew better than anyone else?"

Anamika, a sweet girl with a simple smile across her lips, had come out for the walk with the thought that maybe she could meet him today, but again destiny did not favour her. "Ayushman talked about his aim, but why didn't he talk about his personal life?" thought Anamika. "Would he ever fall in love with me? Can't he see what I can give him? Would I ever get such a chance again to say 'I love you' to him?" she asked herself. Her hopes seemed to have been dashed completely as Ayushman didn't seem aware of her presence even. If he had spoken a word or two in between, things could have been different and there would have been some hope. If only he had allowed her to speak, she could have been in a pleasant state of mind. At least, Ayushman's love would have filled her heart with hope. "But as Ayushman ignores me completely, I need to maintain both his devotion to work and my longing for him."

Technology versus Glamour

* * * * *

Ayushman's intelligence was enough to daunt anyone who thought of standing against him. So it was easy to digest what he had said to Arjun sir just a few minutes ago. And, in fact, he spoke about the same thing in the assembly hall in front of a hundred students the next morning. Thereafter, his teachers came to him to greet him and wish him to do better and keep his spirits up in his aim. Ayushman now had every reason to keep himself confined to his studies as he got engaged in the derivation, ignoring whatever little time he had for being social. He kept everything aside and the only thing which never let him down was his passion for work. Despite being a novice and naïve in his work, he worked for long hours so that he could learn more. He was given the basement of the science block where he could work undisturbed. In fact, it helped him in keeping away from all kinds of disturbances. He even put up a board which said, 'Getting disturbed or disturbing, both can cost one a lot'. Ayushman enjoyed doing his work and even his teachers noticed how his eyes used to acquire vibrant colours and a glow when engaged in the work that he enjoyed. He was trying his level best to give something good to the world and to every citizen who respected science.

He was trying to explore more ways to conduct his experiments and often faced failure and sometimes success. He didn't have a single person to help him and neither did he want anyone as he was an introvert, who liked keeping to himself. He wanted to have someone to inspire him, to instigate him, but who could do it? No one in school had the potential to do it. He needed no one and no one deserved him. However, there were a few teachers and students who were helping him psychologically and they were Anamika, Anshul, Arjun sir and Anuradha ma'am, who were like family members to him by this time.

Arjun sir was handling his thesis and projects; Anuradha ma'am was taking care of his language and editing and Anamika was helping him in curtailing every superfluous segment of his life. Ayushman was told to do his work only and the rest was handled by everyone else. His different style of studying was something which he had acquired himself. His family didn't know about Einstein or what their talented son Ayushman had in his mind.

The best point about him was that his enthusiasm never waned; his interest did not slack and this was because of his exceptionally good mind and inborn skills. His research was on and he decided to cover as many as topics possible for a single man. He was trying to increase his endurance and checking everything that came his way. He knew that he had to be scrupulous as far as his theory was concerned; any miss or mistake would prove very costly to him.

Anamika was no longer a part of his enigmatic life. She knew he could not be disturbed in life or in his work. For this reason, the college had given him a car to make trips up and down. In the private sector, jobs are from 9 a.m. to 5 p.m., in call centres they are from 5 p.m. to 9 a.m., and as far as $E=mc^2$ was concerned, he had to work in two shifts all by himself. And the black car had been given to him just to reduce some of his burden and because of the impressive work he had undertaken. The custom-made car had space to put anything that he wanted as it was so spacious that he could even do his work inside it. It was only meant for him. Since the college had offered him as much comfort as possible, it was now impossible for him to avoid his work. He had to justify the facilities provided to him. He was working hard but the fluctuations were present. A team of senior teachers was told to work with him to help him to be consistent in his task and not lose hope.

Everyone was ready to help him in every possible manner, though he could hardly expect anything from them. He had so much work that he was advised to detach himself from every weakness in life.

How could someone from Class XI or XII handle such a heavy burden? These classes were not enough to have someone like him. All those heavy books like the Pradeep Physics book, the comprehensive Chemistry book, the R.S.

Aggarwal Mathematics book—-not everyone could make out head or tail of these books. At this tender age, youngsters tended to spend time on gossip, smoke/drink, drive cars/bikes at break-neck speed, chat, mail, party, use of social sites, download Hollywood news, flirt. Instead of doing all these things, Ayushman was keen to invent something, to do what had been left incomplete centuries ago. He was keen to earn name and fame, to do something which would keep his name alive. And if he wanted all this so badly, then he surely could come out with his own book on $E=mc^2$.

By this time, Ayushman had only one thing in mind and that was $E=mc^2$. For Anamika it was love and nothing else. "Love is hard to get; harder still when it is purely one-sided. I have to try until I can," Anamika thought.

The pinnacle of success is always hard to reach, he knew. Therefore, he never lost his focus. Both had their own perceptions and their own aims. It was already a month since Ayushman had started doing his work in the basement. Now he was ready with his new lab in the basement. He had learnt so many things at school labs that he tried to build up his own in an almost similar manner and for which he took help from his teachers too.

All kinds of machinery, solutions, chemical reagents, different kinds of lenses, microscopes, meters, test tubes, burettes, flasks, Vernier callipers, screw gauges, telescopes, ampere meters, voltmeters and every other thing was given to him. In fact, he was the only one who had all his stuff at one place as if he were packed up in some scientifically-designed room. 'Home away from a home' was the name of his lab. He decided to do everything he couldn't do in school labs because sometimes they got over-crowded. He was treating all his mistakes as a step to success. He was even striving to overcome every obstacle and defeat every kind of hindrance coming his way.

Ayushman's hard and consistent labour helped to reduce his chances of losing. By seeing him work as a student-scientist, his schoolmates could not help appreciating how well he was fulfilling his responsibilities as a son and citizen. His concentration personified towards fulfilling his aim. He had every reason to be satisfied—a new lab, a new car and a new something could arrive any day. His lab was officially ready, yet it was not inaugurated. The school wanted to invite a high dignitary to open the doors of his lab for the first time. It was not only the inauguration that was important, but a way to expound on the formula publicly. Ayushman had come up with such a discovery that it had to be respected in all its aspects. For this someone high in the hierarchy scale had to be present.

A few days before the inauguration was to take place, the principal and the teachers were see discussing and arguing on whom to invite—a minister, a cricketer, scientist, actor, actress, or someone else, who would happily visit the school and enjoy meeting the students. Cricketer Rahul Dravid was busy in Test matches; Dr A.P.J. Abdul Kalam, Shri Yashwant Sinha and other politicians had already been invited to Scindia; inviting pretty actresses was not found a good option and therefore in the race to the chief guest, an actor won. Who was the actor? Naturally it had to be Shahrukh Khan, who agreed to grace the occasion at Scindia on October 21, 2004. He was to cut the tape of the lab in the opening ceremony while convey the message that even an actor could fit into the sciences and boost the students' morale. Students were brimming with excitement as they wanted to see Ayushman and SRK together. The prospect of seeing two icons together was bound to thrill even the most staid person. The students had been advised in advance that if they wanted to meet them, they had to be best too. Every student was assigned a duty, a task to complete. The teachers were told to keep their collars up; the students were told to be humble and modest; the housemasters/ housemistresses were told to remain vigil; the departments were asked to spruce up; the event managers had to be on their feet and the entire school was washed and cleaned so that it would twinkle like a star under the dark sky.

When the scheduled date arrived, the students could be seen with smiles plastered on their faces. That day everything looked new and even the students seemed new as they had really scrubbed themselves well and worn their best outfits. The garden glistened with dew drops and even the trees were lighted up. Now only Chief Guest had to arrive. On the inauguration day, some students could be seen getting restless and losing patience. After all they waited to see the best in Bollywood, an admirable actor, heartthrob of millions, and a man who endorsed the maximum number of brands, produced the best movies and filed the maximum tax returns. Shahrukh Khan, was about to enter Scindia School.

After two minutes of restless silence, a man wearing a black Armani, seated on the back seat of his convertible BMW was spotted at the gate of Scindia. The crowd went wild with excitement as though God himself had arrived from heaven. What is more, a number of them were keen to be photographed with him than just to see him.

As Scindia had invited Shahrukh, who is more popular as SRK, the organisers had one thing in mind and that was to see a large crowd gather to welcome the Chief Guest. There were teachers, parents of students, relatives of teachers, grandparents of children, local staff along with their families, and many from the whole town of Gwalior to receive the guest. Some of the schoolchildren couldn't get a place to sit, or even catch a glimpse of his dimples. On finding such a large gathering, the principal himself went to SRK's car to escort him amidst tight security. He then guided him to the special sofa placed for him. It was now iike SRK vs Ayushman, a win-win situation for both of them. There was a scientist pitted against a star, technology against glamour, mind versus style, and work against work. On his arrival, the spectators who were observing the rules and staying within the boundary, now broke through to get close to the star. However, with the intervention of teachers and principal some order was restored and proper decorum was observed. At the site of inauguration, the two heroes, Shahrukh and Ayushman were the cynosure of all eyes. Both seemed pleased as punch to receive such adulation. They kept giving fly kisses to the public which had gathered there, answering queries from the mediapersons, smiling gently and posing for photographers, who were busy clicking their cameras. Shahrukh was behaving just as every public figure is expected to do. He participated in all that he was asked to do and performed the inauguration with a scintillating speech. He was simply awesome and did everything in a kingly style all through the function.

SRK began, "I am happy to find an Indian in this country, who has been trying to unravel the mysteries of science lying hidden for decades. I wish him prosperity and my blessings are with him. I hope he will achieve whatever he wants."

The function was short and crisp as SRK had to return to Mumbai that very night. He had other commitments to fulfil apart from shooting for his upcoming movie, 'Paheli', directed by Amol Palekar and help in the promotion of 'Veer-Zara', a Yash Chopra film. That night, the two dignitaries, Shahrukh and Ayushman left everybody thrilled to the core. Next morning, Ayushman was being looked upon by the students as the star of the school because the movie star, Shahrukh Khan, had already left the night before. He was now being counted among the 'biggies'. His popularity was however not appreciated by everyone; there were some boys who were fuming within to see him win everyone's heart.

As only a few months were left for Ayushman to appear for the Class XII Board exam and as he did not want to displease even his worst critics, he decided to ask

Arjun sir and the principal to allow him to speak from the stage for a couple of minutes. They permitted him and gave him the freedom to say whatever he wanted. Like everyone, he too entered the assembly hall and after saying the morning prayers, he was asked to speak. As he went up on to the stage, he became somewhat nervous and asked himself, "Would this talk on the stage satisfy me or the others? Do I have any other option? Perhaps, no."

He began his speech, "In the initial months at Scindia School, where I learnt how to take my steps and build new dreams of being a scientist, from then itself, things started changing for me. I had never expected to become addicted to the system but I did become. I have done a lot of things here and am still left with some work to do. In fact, I am due to clear all apprehensions related to my work, but all this is possible only if you bolster me in my work. Though you have done it so far, there are still some people who are not in favour of me. I wish to state I have come to recognise myself only when I came here. Did I make a mistake? If I was regularly attending my classes, did I make any mistake? Was honing of my skills a wrong step?"

"I have always believed that bad times never prevail for long. However, I seldom smell a fragrance of good days in my life. Why is it so? I am devoting all my time to reach the top but is it wrong? Am I harming you? Why is it that some of you won't let me to do my work? What would you all, who do not like me, get by putting obstacles in my work? You will not gain any profit by doing this. I have been helping you all in your work since I came here, so don't I deserve the same? I always keep warm relations with everyone and keep alleviating the problems of others who approach me for help. Have I ever refused to offer my services to any of you? Then why can't you all give me your unstinted support? Is that too much that I am asking of you?

"I am completely zapped at the fact that why should anyone amongst you have anything against me? All I want is to do my job well, without being disturbed. If you feel embarrassed to associate with me, then leave me. I will never be kicked out from here until I want it that way," he asserted with force.

His words led to pin-drop silence and even his critics were seen squirming with shame and become red in the face. Since all of them were seated together, one could notice the shame written on their face. They all were sitting in one row and kept looking at each other till one of them had tears of embarrassment in their eyes. "If he had wanted, he could have announced out names in front of everyone, but he didn't," said the boy, choked nearly with tears.

"Ayushman is much better than us," mumbled a second boy among them.

"We need to know how to respect him, rather than to despise him," said a third with some force.

By the time Ayushman completed his speech, his critics were filled with disdain and realised that whatever they had done was wrong. Aysuhman climbed down the stage to walk towards the exit gate. His firm and steady steps were conveying his message in no uncertain terms.

He glanced with a crooked smile playing on his lips as he noticed some of the boys staring at him and feeling sorry.

He had topped in Class XI tests held in August 2004 and had been presented the captain's shirt for the science stream, for the many projects completed, for his ever-readiness to help fellow students and what not. When the boys entered Class XII, they got busy chalking new ideas, new routes, new careers, but there was nothing new for Ayushman to chart. There were other career options available that time but none was sufficient enough to allure him. "Only the class has changed, but the aim remains the same," said Ayushman to everyone who came to seek his advice on what to choose.

Marks scored in Class XII play an indispensable part in one's life but even this did not affect him. All he wanted was to reach the epilogue of his experiment and win laurels from eminent scientists of the day. On getting promoted to Class XII, he was appointed school captain and it caused no surprise as it was expected. On his appointment day, he was asked to give a speech as he had given before, but this time it was to be as a captain.

"Everyone was good to me and I expect the same attitude in future also. I am thankful to my teachers for their unstinted support in all that I have done and without whose cooperation I could not have done much. However, it all points to the fact that one person alone cannot bring about a change. I need your cooperation in this and expect you to do the same also. Thus, I seek your help in my experiments and practical work at every step that I take henceforth. Do your best and stand by your convictions," he exhorted them.

This time as soon as he completed his speech, all of them stood up to assure him of every possible help and support that he may need in achieving his aim. He knew he had to do his best and produce worthy results so that students would look up to him as their role model. Moreover, as the captain, he had to shoulder the extra responsibility and deliver the goods to the best of his ability. The day he became the captain, his housemaster invited him to participate in every discussion pertaining to their house.

His work was progressing smoothly till he was asked to attend a science fair, which was to be conducted at the Scindia Kanya Vidyalya. Though not happy with this disruption, as was his wont, he put in all his time and effort to make the event a success. Not only he, many other good science students were invited to participate on the occasion. All of them were part of the same branch and had been with him since they started their respective school lives. They were told to remain strong and vigilant because all sorts of attractions could have made them shirk their duty. One of the students asked very smartly, "Who will escort the guests around the fair?"

A teacher replied, "I told you, the girls will."

"Then can you advise where to look and what to avoid? Should we concentrate on the experiments or somewhere else?" the mischievous student continued.

"Listen, you all are invited because you are the best, so behave properly," replied a teacher rather tersely, before turning and walking out of the room.

Ayushman and his friends collected the complete schedule giving details of the work assigned to each of the students and how they had to conduct it. He was rather serious as it meant trying to squeeze in time for putting up a good show besides attending to his research. He was asked to attend to moderate in a debate where both girls and boys were to participate. No prior preparation could be done as everyone had to speak extempore.

Ayushman's bus arrived at the right time and as he stepped out the bus, he saw more than a hundred girls cheering and waving frantically at him. His work at Scindia was already known in the town. In fact, he was more popular there than anyone else. His work, his achievements, his published papers, his objective, all had won him accolades and due recognition. His bus stopped exactly in front of SKV's gate and from there he had to walk to the principal's office for collecting further details. As it was a bit further away from the main gate, Ayushman had difficulty in negotiating his way through the large crowd of girls cheering him. Since it was difficult to find his way through the crowd, a car was sent to pick him up from the gate to take him to the principal's office. Once he had reached the office, he directly went to the room where the debate was scheduled to be held.

The principal of SKV was with him all the time while attending to the arrangements too. Many boys stood to provide security and a few more waited to greet him. By the time he entered the room, the whole crowd turned to look at Ayushman walking past them on to the stage. A majority of them had only heard about him but not seen him. Before he could even sit down, a number of questions were shot at him. He tried answering their queries to the best of his ability but he longed to sit down while speaking. At one point of time he felt so stressed out that he thought he would have to call it off, but through sheer will power, he stuck on till the end. After a while, the curtains were rolled up and two girls came forward to host the proceedings. The topic for the debate was **'Expanding horizons of science are fatal or fruitful for the world'**.

The topic was initiated by Ayushman who spoke in favour of the subject. He began, "I am completely in favour of this topic as we all belong to the same field. We are gathered here in this scientifically-crowded place. So are we commiting a mistake? Can this act prove fatal to this world? Are we wrong to choose science as a branch? I would like to say that if we are successful in this world, then will there be any point in asking me a question regarding this?"

"Now, you tell me, what is wrong with our schooling system to go from IITs and science subjects to other branches. Are we being unfair to mankind? Is studying science in school wrong for mankind? No, all these efforts which we are making right now, whatever we are studying, whatever we are going through will be contributing towards growth of science only. So, are we being cruel to mankind? We will enter B-tech after a year followed by higher studies like M-tech, and Ph. D to reach the higher domains of science. Whatever we do, we shall be contributing directly/indirectly to science only. We all realise that if we misuse our technology, we shall do harm to mankind. But if we are properly educated and have our feet firmly on the ground, then why should any destructive thought arise in our mind? I am not trying to boast about what we do at Scindia. My concern is to do good by keeping good in mind and making this earth a better place to live on. So, are we fatal to mankind or to this world?"

"Now, tell me when you start your B-tech, some of you may design software, some may come forward to design an ATM machine which doesn't require a password but needs a handprint to start so that even a farmer can operate it. The coming generation will play with micro chips; they will make things which have chips inside or they will come out with the fastest micro-controller. Biotechnology will design a drug for any disease and scientists will come up with potent ideas to improve the soil fertility or make the world disease free. They will try to curb all hazardous diseases from spreading and taking away precious lives. So, are we bad?"

"Let's talk about the new trends now. Nowadays smoking has become a part of everyone's life or a definite need. Let's suppose a man is used to smoking more than three packets per day and lives with the dread of developing throat cancer is unable to curb his urge. Soon we will have no fear of throat cancer because we would have discovered new drugs to stop cell multiplication. Are we harming mankind with this technology?"

"No, on the contrary, we are saving our own generation through our knowledge of science. The same is true for habitual drinkers. They can even get their liver transplanted in the event of an emergency. I think we are life savers."

"Now to cite a very simple instance, some of film stars have gone in for hair transplant and are able to continue as young heroes, while earning a lot. In case someone has conjoined twins, then doctors will easily separate them and save them. We have so many advantages of technology nowadays that we can even save a premature baby, detect cancer in its initial stages and we can fix bones too. In fact, our icons, Amitabh Bachchan, Sachin Tendulkar, Shahrukh Khan have had some minor and major problems to be fixed in their bodies, and they are now leading a very normal life. So are we misusing science?"

"We are using science like never before. In short, every step that we take in science can be harmful or worthwhile. We have to understand both these aspects of science and then go ahead to use it for beneficial purposes. Try to do well and prevent any wrong from happening."

This speech earned him a standing ovation from everyone. His every word contained a message and did not go waste on those who understood him well. The appreciation raised his heartbeats, increased his pulse beats and sent blood racing to his head with pride. Filled with excitement, he gave warm hugs to everyone sitting or standing near him. The principal of SKV escorted him to the spot where the fair had been organised by his friends.

In fact, he was kept constantly on his toes as a volley of queries was showered on him.

It was here when he met Prof. Paul Smith, who later became his tutorial guide. He said, “I too was invited to SKV as I was a deserving candidate just as Ayushman is. In fact, I was told to meet him as a part of the normal procedure before meeting him formally in school. I met him as any other spectator in my normal attire. We discussed the point of his debate and I even told him about certain points which could have been included. But as it was an extempore attempt, he put up a good show. In extempore debates, one hardly gets time to think of anything.”

“It was because of him school took my interview in the beginning of 2004. I am Prof. Paul Smith, retired from work and taking rest by being at home in Gwalior.” When we first shook hands, I could feel his intensity and integrity. I could see everything clearly in his eyes and before I could leave SKV, I told him about my interview and about joining as project executive of $E=mc^2$. We were both thrilled to bits and parted for our separate destinations. He went ahead to learn more about the fair while I returned to my room as I already knew about the projects put up on display. Ayushman is no longer the master of his own life; it is the others who have decided his destiny. I feel if Ayushman had not met me or anyone among us, then his life surely would have taken a different turn.”

Love Enters Surreptitiously

* * * * *

Many projects had been put up at the science fair and these were displayed artistically as never seen before. It was very pleasant to see the way the students had worked together to put up the show. Unluckily, Ayushman and his friends could not devote as much time as they would have desired. In any case he was enjoying, seeing everything, moving from department to department before his feet carried him to the computer lab. He began to ask a girl about the details on her project. He was deeply engrossed in learning about the model when his eyes suddenly fell on a girl standing at a distance from him. He immediately fell in love with her. Love at first sight had happened. History had been repeated.

Ayushman in love? How is this possible? Are we hallucinating or is this true?

He had fallen in love with a girl whom he had never met before in his whole life. Again it was a case of love at first sight. He kept staring at her without blinking his eyes. He left the girl with whom he was discussing the project and made his way towards this comely stranger. "Scientists are also humans. They have a heart too," Ayushman thought, as if defending his behaviour to himself. "Surely they too can fall in love as they are also needed to carry out the reproduction process. But is love only meant for reproduction purposes?"

Let's find out.

He suddenly became aware of his rude and brusque behaviour towards the girl who was explaining the model and turned back towards her to ask for her forgiveness. But the girl didn't reply as she had become green with jealousy at the centre of his attention. "I don't know what you think about me, but how can I be ignored like this?" she asked him.

Ayushman had no answer and found himself completely taken aback. "Okay, you don't want to forgive me? Alright, at least tell me her name if you know it," Ayushman begged of her.

But the girl behaved rather churlishly. She ignored him completely just as he had ignored her. But Ayushman kept asking her the same thing. When he kept on insisting, she told him that the girl's name was Sneya.

Ayushman found himself in a strange world where dreams run high and all looks bright and green. Just by repeating her name within his lips he began to acquire a strange thrill. He felt as though he had won Aishwarya Rai. From the moment he set his eyes on Sneya, he felt completely mesmerised and all his formulae started running wild in his mind. Such a madness had never possessed him earlier. He could never feel satisfied for the urge to see her beauty again and again rose in his mind like a disease. Henceforth wherever he saw her, his eyes dogged her and due to his inherent shyness, he was not able to utter a single word in front of her. In fact, he never found the right opportunity to accost her and have a heart to heart talk with her. Nevertheless, he was enjoying every moment of fleeting thoughts that crossed his mind every now and then. He began to feel the vibes of his love in the air around him. "Why is love so intangible sometimes?" Ayushman thought.

He heard an announcement being made, asking the visitors to get seated on their respective buses as the time of the function was coming to an end. The announcement had come rather late for Ayushman, who was already head over heels in love. Had it been announced earlier, he could have saved himself from falling in love. By now, lots of things had changed, including his priorities. Now he was no longer the person who always heard his mind, but a person who had become a slave of his heart. When he got back into his bus, he knew he would have to answer many questions as he had became late.

"What all did you see in the science fair, Ayushman?" asked his instructor.

Ayushman replied, "I saw my life today, sir."

"I never expected this kind of an answer or reaction from you, Ayushman," replied the teacher in a tone of reprimand.

As Ayushman was completely technological-savvy, the teacher thought maybe he had found his life in the experiments. Therefore, he didn't say much and ordered the bus driver to take them back to the fort.

Ayushman took his seat in the bus but his eyes kept darting to the entrance gate of SKV in the desperate hope of catching one more glance of her. As it was an air-conditioned bus, Ayushman couldn't leave the window open or obtain a proper view of the scene outside. He again adjusted himself on his seat and started looking out but failed to see any sign of her. If only he could have told her before he entered the bus, he could have got a few moments to spend with her. He was looking at the gate so desperately that it led others to wonder what was wrong with him! He kept looking at the same point till SKV was left far behind and out of focus.

It became tough for Ayushman to obliterate thoughts about her and it became still harder to wipe out the memories of her endearing face. He reached his school but with only a part of his body and mind. The rest he had already gifted to his lady love. He lost his seriousness and became a dreamer, forever lost in his thoughts. He was now no more a scientist but an emotional human being. His statements and answers in class were intriguing both to his teachers and fellow students.

Though Ayushman was worried about his incomplete work, he somehow could not concentrate on his task, try as he might. He tried many times to restore his thoughts and feelings to the task on hand, but his heart refused to budge.

It is at this stage that my role begins. I came to the fort to see his life and the experiments which he had done so far. I was glad to see his work. Most of the theories were complete and so was his thesis. I went to see his lab, his room and his academic block and even took a ride in his stylish black car. I wondered why they had not given him a spaceship instead! Then, at last, I sat next to him and asked him about his life and told him, "My boy, don't tell me any lie and answer my questions right to the point so long as you are with me."

Thus Ayushman told me everything, including the story about his family in Delhi, Arjun sir, the physics teacher, Anuradha ma'am, the English teacher, Anamika Agarwal and Anshul Agarwal—his best pals and about his other friends too. And then in the end he revealed about Sneya. He said he had fallen in love with her and could not live without seeing her.

I didn't feel like commenting anything on his personal life as I was there at the fort for professional duty only. Next morning, I joined him officially. Scindia always wanted to have someone to help Ayushman as the administration was more curious than me about his experiments and his success so far. Now Ayushman had two things to solve—first, the mystery of the formula and second, find out the meaning of falling in love with her.

"Either I am good enough to tell you about Scindia School or I am not. But listen, Ayushman, I know about this school and only after finding about the school have I come here. I do have lots of money and there is no need for me to go anywhere. Yet I came to work as a project executive on $E=mc^2$. And now see what you are doing with your life. First, it's been long since you came here, so I don't need to tell you about its charm. Second, there is no need to describe it because Scindia School is a reputed school which students join not only to study but to develop an all-round personality. Students generally get so much by the life at Scindia that they hardly visit their homes until they have completed their schooling. The school has swimming pools, riding fields, football-cricket-hockey fields, basketball courts, elocution-debate halls, big auditorium to perform open air performances, highly talented teachers and a wholesome life. However, with many children clamouring for admission here, there is a lot of competition nowadays and children have to come out to do something, to learn something. I am sure your parents thought the same when they sent you here. You have undoubtedly lived on your own in the school, but what has happened now? Why has your interest waned? Scindia School is like a line which once written on your forehead cannot be erased. Automatically your importance gets enhanced if you know, how to encash it. You must have heard that a 'well' never comes near a thirsty person; one has to go near it to quench one's thirst. Similarly, you must know how to grab the opportunities given by Scindia and make the most of them. You have to respect the love which they have for you. They have a lot of expectations from you as a scientist. So, Ayushman, if love is nc longer a constraint for you, then can you start your work at a quicker pace? In fact, it would teach you how to live in the scientifically-driven world of $E=mc^2$," said I to him to motivate him anew.

He began to work with me but my words couldn't work on him as well as I had expected. He was still thinking about her as he was deeply in love.

One day he said to Anshul, his best friend, "If I were to send a letter to her, maybe she would say 'yes'."

After some discussions, he decided to send her something instead. "What about a letter? I hardly know how to write a love letter?" he thought. "What to do now? Whom should I approach?" He kept on debating in his mind as to whom to ask for the favour. He had to find a person who was aware of his feelings and emotions and pure in his or her heart also. The only name which cropped up in his mind was that of Anamika Agarwal. He wanted to approach a girl who had loved him from the bottom of her heart and who could contact the girl whose glimpse he had caught. "I should send a letter to Anamika requesting her to write a letter on my behalf to Sneya," he decided.

Letter for Anamika

* * * * *

Words can be conveyed by quoting lines written in one or two golden sentences by eminent writers but for me it is difficult to compute the tenor of our relationship which we have shared till now. It seems as if we have been friends since we came in this world. I wonder how much you have understood the crux of this relationship but I have understood it perfectly. Since the very start, I was very sharp towards you but you kept a equilibrium and never took it amiss. Sometimes I feel it is because of you that I am here on this planet. In fact, credit goes to my parents even. I am too glad to be having a kindly soul like you as a friend who never attempts to muzzle, never gets frenzied and always delivers solace and comfort to me. Many have told me how to achieve success, but you have told me a direct way to success. The elation I feel on seeing you cannot be put down in words.

I know you have done so much for me but today I am asking you for a favour. I have the temerity to say something to you as I feel we are close to each other and can divulge my feelings freely to you. A few days ago, I visited the science fair at SKV and there I fell in love with a girl. It was there that I realised how much I loved her but couldn't say anything to her. Now I want you to do something for me. I want you to write something on my behalf as I am not so good at expressing my feelings. I have gone mad since I have seen her and now I want her to love me. She didn't see me that day, but from my side the emotions of love abound for her. You have done a lot for me, but can I ask you for one last favour? I know this would be easy for a girl like you to write who is filled with emotions. Don't take me wrongly. Just try to do what I am saying and this would help me a lot.

You are an indispensable part of my life and even if you fail to do the needful, we will remain as we have been so far.

From

Ayushman

When Anamika received this letter, she couldn't believe her eyes and started screaming loudly at every corner of her house. She couldn't control herself on receiving Ayushman's letter. She began to wonder, "Was I ever a part of his life? Should I expect something still worse than this to come? Did I deserve this from him? See, what he has given me!"

She began to shout and rant and her voice became heavy as though she had lost all control over herself. She got up from the floor and while mumbling to herself, ran from one room to another. Once she shouted so loudly that it made everyone to step out from their house and check what had gone wrong. The servant of the house called up her mother, who rushed home from work and tried to pacify her and offer some solace. When completely dejected, she fell on her Mom's shoulders and dozed off to sleep. Her mother kept thinking what she could do to console her daughter.

Next morning, Anamika woke up from her sleep, but in no better a mood than what she was in the previous night. "Who should I blame for all this?" said she to herself. "This is an exceptionally fierce blow aimed at my heart. I gave every second of my life to him, never asking for any justification though. I faced periods of extreme tension and stress in my life and sometimes I became completely irascible just because of him. He would just go to the stage to say whatever he wanted, whenever he wanted and I listened to every word of his as though it was nothing but the gospel truth. Now what should I do? Should I go on to the stage and tell everyone how he has hurt me? I have cried many times, behaved boorishly towards my Mom because of him, even bunked classes, disobeyed my teachers, and what do I get in return? He has left me in a knotty situation which is not of my kind and gone off to spin dreams of Sneya. How should I react now? Should I pat his back? Is my love false?" She kept asking all these questions from herself till night appeared.

Then she looked up at the sky and cried, "Why are these stars shining yet? Who gave them the permission to shine when I am in pain?"

But who was there among the stars to see her pain? Her smiling countenance lost its softness forever and she felt as a piece of rot. It was the biggest tragedy of her life. We often lose our lives whenever any catastrophe strikes. Similarly with her, instead of losing her life, she lost her love. Her Mom had no answer for this and as her studies had already suffered a lot, it seemed this was the last nail in her coffin. She could neither get him nor attend to her studies. Her life was as good as over. She had never expected this to happen. She had to put to end to her dolorous life and their relationship cruelly. Before ending her relationship forever, she looked back on every second of her time spent with Ayushaman and kept recalling the same moments while writing a letter to him. With tears streaming down her face, she continued to write her letter. Totally heartbroken, she somehow managed to write what she felt simply because it was for Ayushman. She could recall every walk, every class, every evening, and everything that they shared in the days now gone past. She used her own experience to write the letter for him.

How could anybody be so sweet and humble to someone whom she had loved and who was now asking her to help him with another girl? As an afterthought, she decided to help him despite the near-fatal blow she had received from him. Really, she was as good as to any other 'big shot' deserving celebrity status by getting a wax replica made of herself and placed in Madame Tussaud's museum in London. She deserved at least this small award for all her sacrifices. After doing what she could to give vent to her feelings—she shouted, she cried, she wandered aimlessly, she kept herself empty-stomach, she kept herself locked, she hated love, she abused herself and Sneya, she rang up Ayushman's housemaster to seek his permission to talk to him.

She told Ayushman on the phone, "I have already started writing the letter for you. I am trying to create an impression on her heart so that she would begin to feel the same way towards you as you do towards her. In the end, I can only say that I will try my level best to bind your heart with hers through my words. However, all you need is to wait right now," and disconnected. She was not in a state to continue the conversation as she was likely to break down any moment. Her Mom stood silently behind her, witnessing her daughter's sorrow and feeling miserable for her.

Ayushman had now to find a person who could drop his letter at SKV. He wanted someone to establish close links within SKV or with someone who knew how to go across the fence. He feared being caught and therefore did not do anything himself. On seeing him in this weak state, one felt that all of a sudden Ayushman had lost all his smartness and become weak by falling in love with a girl at SKV. It has rightly been said that when a person falls in love, he keeps finding someone else to do things on his behalf. But if this is true, then why is it that this is seen prior to a person's marriage? Why is it that you expect your friends to do good things for you so that your love life may blossom but then why not allow them to do things after your marriage too? While Ayushman was frantically searching for a person to carry his letter, Anamika was trying to couch her words in flowery language so that the letter would please Ayushman's friend.

After a few weeks, Anamika rang up Ayushman to ask him to collect his letter from her residence. This was just an excuse on her part to see him for one last time as she used to do when they enjoyed their junior classes in each other's company. She knew that once the letter reached the other girl, her own life would undergo a radical change. She was helping her love to get his love. Unfortunately, the writer of the letter who had spent her precious years with the sender as a lover/friend/companion had not let him down and was writing the letter on his behalf to one who herself didn't know anything about the sender or the writer.

This sacrifice seemed bigger than any other immolation bid made in any century. The letter that Anamika received from Ayushman's so-called love ran as follows:

Dear Anamika,

We are in a world of fluctuating feelings and emotions—a world where we seldom get what we want. Hence even to see the sun rise is to expect the unexpected to happen. The same thing happened with me when I first saw you at the function—stable, lively, jocular and brimming with happiness. I have seen many who feel tormented when they see unforgettable beauties near them. However, I felt very light when I saw you at SKV and then and there I decided that you were meant for me only. I didn't approach you, though.

I hardly know anything about you, yet I feel I have known you since long. I don't know how my eyes landed on you and once they did, they got stuck on you and I kept staring at you throughout the entire function. All I know is that on seeing you for a few hours alone without knowing each other but finding every fraction of a second as unforgettable and indelible, I write this letter in the hope that I will receive a suitable reply from you. I have spent my days/nights dreaming about you and remembering your smiling face while talking to your friends. As it would have been improper, I didn't approach you. I wonder whether I would ever get a girl like you!

But I feel that those who know you and are close to you are extremely lucky.

Sneya, truly speaking,

1st glance, I saw you, you were a stranger to me.

2nd glance, I saw you, you were stranger to me.

3rd glance, I saw you, I fell in love with you despite being a stranger only. You too might have felt something by now, but I would recommend you to feel the purity with which everything has been ordained.

Your winsome smile at the function left me completely fascinated by you. It is great to be respected. However, it was your charm which made me stare at you. I am a bit far from you but trust me, every day I remember you. I seldom see myself because every day I want to see you. Words are less important than feelings but feelings cannot be printed on paper as they don't have any observable physical entity. Therefore ,I am forced to send you this letter. Maybe this letter will help you gauge my feelings properly than via words. Whenever I think of you, I become confused. Whenever I don't think of you, then I become still more confused. You cannot imagine how confused I am right now, but truly at the function you were looking like a star, which is still shining in my heart. Your eyes looked enticing and your sweet smile acted like magic in my life. You are like a drop which alone is sufficient to fill millions of potholes and fill everyone's life with happiness. Your charisma is stupendous and brings hope for thousands of people whose dreams are yet to be fulfilled. Really, your beauty is something beyond words and you cannot be compared with any existing or non-existing thing. I know I should have spoken all this before only at the function, but I was not able to remove my eyes from you at that time. You might have heard all such fanciful sentences before even, but let me tell you, I am not like them.

I could only stand and stare at you without saying a word and my feelings are strong and pure, trust me. You can stop yourself from coming near me, but you cannot stop me from loving you.

I don't have any experiment by which I can prove my love. All I know is that I am in love. How I wish you too were to feel the same.

Love

Ayushman

This letter appeared to have been written by Anamika for Ayushman only, but actually it was meant for Sneya written by Anamika on Ayushman's behalf. On reading this letter, even Ayushman couldn't believe that Anamika could write so well. Little did he know that she could write thus because of her feelings for him, just as Ayushman had for Sneya.

"How could a person who has never been in love write this kind of sentimental letter," wondered Ayushman on receiving this letter from Anamika. So, this letter was sent to Sneya via Anshul (the only person who had friends at SKV). But Ayushman lost some of his boldness and turned tense after sending the letter because he did not receive any response for months. He waited for a week and gradually his self-confidence started giving way and he lost all hope. He could hardly pay attention to his work. Therefore, I had to pull him up and gave him a dressing down for being irregular at work. Here too Anamika came forward to help him. She was the one who had brought new hope in his life, no matter what he had given her. But Ayushman became a recluse and stopped talking. He began to stay in seclusion as though he preferred his own company than somebody else's. His long and withdrawn face drew the attention of his schoolmates too. They tried to revive his interest in his project and stood by him like strong pillars.

"How long can scientists be kept away from work?" asked his friends. Ayushman had plenty of friends ready to vouch for him and help him out in times of need. Thus, very reluctantly and after a lot of persuasion and cajoling, he returned to his work and decided to ignore the importance of his letter. He started again from where he had left off and even tried to take charge of his emotions and suffering. This was all due the unstinted support of his friends. I was happy too when I saw his recovery. We both started working again with full devotion and interest and began to draw closer to achieving success. On seeing him regain his confidence, I started going on my foreign trips to gather more related information on $E=mc^2$.

He was lucky to get me as an instructor as I was the only one who had plenty of sources abroad and I was happy to do whatever I could for him. He had his own knowledge and theories while I had my own. We had a good understanding of each other's capability and worked together, keeping this point in our mind. Ayushman was able to do more with my help and I was satisfied with that. We worked till late in the night and return absolutely tired out after a long day. The homework which I gave him and my strict discipline were among the other things responsible for keeping him far from his love life and consequent distractions. However, he had not forgotten about his letter to her. No response had been received so far.

I brought from many universities in UK the information that would have helped us in our research. Every university willingly came forward to help me as I was the one who had given them so many years of my life and lived as a family member there. In fact, the universities were only too happy to help a child who could think of taking up something like this. Some of the leading universities were Manchester, Stanford, Liverpool, Kent, Aberdeen, Leicester and Nottingham. Even Ayushman appreciated my labour and therefore took to working like a maniac on his project.

While working together, not many problems came our way. Ayushman was slogging practically but I could see he still waited for the letter. We were behaving that all was well but I knew how desperate he was to receive a line or two from her. We were working together and Anamika was the only person who could visit us but she preferred to stay at home. She even stopped attending her classes and took rest from school sessions by submitting false medical certificates. She was in a foul mood and completely unhappy with her life. One or two of her friends, who saw her unknowingly, found her roaming with a dirty appearance, filthy clothes, matted hair, oily face, parched lips and an empty stomach. This was in stark contrast to what Ayushman possessed—a sophisticated lifestyle, a large laboratory, a luxury car, research meetings with me, and exposure at the global level. Anamika felt as though she had been left far behind. Did they have any similarity? Did they share anything in common as they used to earlier?

Ayushman cannot be blamed for it is expected of every scientist to show more fidelity towards his work rather than anything else. He had understood what life meant but Anamika had to fathom this yet. She would often get into arguments over this issue with him and their never-ending altercations made them more diffident to each other. Her Mom tried to pacify her just as any other Mom would do, but she seemed to have forgotten to obey like every child. Anamika thought that if they couldn't be lovers, then why be friends even?

"I am the one who wrote his love letter and as such he should have the decency to show some courtesy to me. It is a big favour that I have done to him," she felt. She began to feel cheated and lost all her perceptions. She would lock herself up in her room for hours and not would no come out. Many a times her Mom had to call a doctor to dissuade her from staying all alone in her room. She even kept more servants to keep an eye on her activities. Ayushman was unaware of all this, engrossed as he was with his experiments. Anamika was confused due to him; Ayushman was confused due to the delay in reply, and I was confused as to how scientists could ever have love marriages. I had to face a lot of flak on his behalf as my duty was to keep an eye on his activities so that he would not wander from the right path.

In between, the speed of our work slackened when Ayushman received the response from Sneya, though she took very long over it. He was nevertheless thrilled to receive an answer, though I was not happy at this development. "What would happen if the answer was to be a 'no'? What would I do then?" I thought. "If anything goes awry, then Ayushman would lose his stability and sanity which he had just recovered," thought I.

Ayushman was working in his lab when he was told to come out as Anshul had brought a letter from Sneya. Ayushman, for a moment shocked, became so ebullient that he nearly jumped to the heavens. He came out at the speed of a hurricane while the others debated on the contents of the letter as per their own experience.

"My hands are shaking. I think you better open it," said Ayushman rather recklessly to Anshul. He told Anshul to open it as he didn't have any strength left to face his destiny. Everyone told him to open it himself as it was his first love letter, but Ayushman was not prepared to touch it even. In fact, he didn't see it himself, plagued as it was by some unknown fear. "Maybe the address will get changed, or the words will show back, or lines will appear as if someone was flying a kite, or the colour of the ink would fade, and in the end, only a blank paper would be left," thought Ayushman, apprehensive of even touching the envelope. Scientists too can become superstitious, unbelievable.

Anshul didn't read the letter verbally as he was keen to read between the lines though to no effect. By the time he finished the letter, he had lost all his interest and he gave the letter to Anamika. Anamika began to cry inconsolably before she could finish reading. Anshul and I stood near the tree and were waiting for the apple to fall again. Just kidding...

As it was too hot, we were using the tree's branches to obtain shade. I advised him to get back with his work as it was too late for him to give a response. I had advised him a number of times not to get entangled with one girl and be friends with many others, but my advice seemed to have fallen upon deaf ears. "Do not remember her as she has gone forever. You better do what you have been doing for years. Maybe once your aim gets noticed worldwide, then you may become bigger than her. Until that time comes, you need to concentrate only on you work," said I to Ayushman.

Senya's response was totally different from the others' expectations. After reading the letter, Ayushman felt completely heartbroken and so did his other friends. They could no decipher the girl's intentions. They all knew very little about the writer's feelings till they had read every line. Apparently, every line of Sneya's letter smote everyone's mind and heart badly. After reading it, they all concluded that her main objective was to show that a never-seen-person is unable to ignite anything in anyone. By this time, every reader would have already guessed what would be the answer.

If not, then read on and you may be able to tell whether to cry or laugh.

A Rude Jolt

* * * * *

The letter from Sneya read as follows:

To Ayushman

This letter has two parts—the first will make you feel embarrassed while the second will make you feel better. I am considering both the aspects—cruelty and humanity. I do not want to sound rude, but if I do so, then I will repent it later. You can ask if this is to be the reply to your love letter. Then buddy, my reason to write is this is to make you realise how a sane person actually reacts when she/he faces some asinine act as you have committed.

CRUELTY: I don't know you exactly, though I have heard about you many times, but seriously I am not like those who stood at the gate when you came like a hero. In fact, I was not there, as I was busy handling the tasks assigned to me for the function. I don't know how you would feel or react to this letter, but I am taking it very seriously. I came here at SKV to study only. Maybe you joined Scindia for wasting your time over such bull-shit. I wonder how you could have become a student of a reputed school like Scindia? I think you shall be sent to the lunatic asylum if you continue with such soppy stuff. When I read your letter I was shocked, more so because here I was expecting some feedback on the function held at SKV, but instead I receive a 'love letter' from you. I am still wondering what all I might have done in the computer-lab that made you go crazy. If you call this 'love at first sight', then sorry, I am not interested. There are lots of guys in the town who pass by, but do I get engaged to everyone? I am still unable to place my finger on that expression of mine which could have made you fall in love with me. Listen, I am not interested in these things at this age or at any age. We had invited you to have fun, but scientifically. We didn't expect any one of you falling in love with anyone here—mentally.

I agree that the unexpected does happen in life but this was more than what I did expect. As of now, I am not left with any other choice except to reject you.

HUMANITY: It takes someone a solitary look to fall in love with someone. I am happy that you had many at the function but what about me? You tell me how I can say something to you when I didn't see you? I know you and I are in the same boarding school and will not be able to meet before Class XII comes to an end. So, dude, either keep patience till we meet next or forget it all like a dream.

From

Sneya

The only thing he could say at that moment was "whom I detest most is none else but myself." He admitted this to all the bystanders. His voice was tinged with a profound sense of sorrow as though he had been totally broken into innumerable pieces. This was the month of December 2004.

The letter was enough to rob him of all his happiness. He looked as if he was on his knees, under the sky, with his hands out, as if begging for mercy after receiving a blow at his heart. He had never expected such a blow. His eyes filled with sorrow and self-pity for having been reduced to a bumbling fool. Here he had been awaiting her reply with a fond hope and anticipation but what did he get? Brickbats and insult to smother him into asphyxia. He tried to find himself a love, but got hatred and humiliation instead. His friends were very unhappy at the letter and could think of doing nothing except to curse Sneya and her odious act. The letter left him speechless and upset. What a name he earned for himself when the entire Scindia School got to know of the letter!

"If such a letter can be sent by Sneya, what else can we expect from her?" said Anshul to Ayushman as if to console him. As a matter of fact, Ayushman didn't take the letter amiss; on the contrary, when one's love is so overpowering, a person becomes obdurate enough to face anything.

This was the case of Anamika too. Anamika was finding herself in the same situation as Ayushman happened to be in now. What could it be called?

Ayushman went into deep depression and was given to sleeping on an empty stomach as if to test how much cruelty he could withstand. He who used to solve everyone else's problems found that when it came to his own problems, there was nobody to solve them for him. He was in a state of complete mayhem. He was fighting with himself since he couldn't find his lady-love. He felt that he had lost both in love and in his work too. Ayushman and I had been given some tentative dates to submit the experiment but now it seemed that our work would take longer. His performance, work, speed, everything had lost their charm and quality for him. I told him many times to expedite his work but my efforts seemed futile.

I said to him one day, "Ayushman, we are already underway to completing our project. We have taken hefty loans, registered our names to keep ourselves updated about everything, used manpower from the school, called many experienced junior staff to look after petty things, approached sources from abroad and everyone is praying for both of us so that we may win some day. Ever since we have started, everyone has helped us a lot. I think we owe it to them to do well." I said this in order to remind him of his responsibility and get over his love life. "If you give up, then millions of hopes will get shattered."

It did have some effect as I noticed him attending to his pending work with fervour and zeal. He did show the same passion but still he was working. Later, he himself realised that his work was not taking him in the direction in terms of its completion. He was aware that everything was wrong with him but his determination was deserting him from further work. However, he was striving again and again to be on the podium, but every time he lacked something somehow.

I went and met the principal and told him that Ayushman seemed too tense and needed a break. "Send him home for a better ambience," I suggested.

The principal saw my point and readily agreed to send him for a short time. "He will not be called back before he recovers completely. We will wait till that time comes," he said.

Slowly everyone at the fort began to feel the same way but could do nothing. In fact, they were least interested to discuss anything to do with SKV. They were not supposed to do or say anything against Sneya and therefore they kept their mouth shut.

Ayushman was sent home as he was mentally ill. Doctors advised him to take a long break so that he could be free of all tensions. He was not able to understand anything about her. He was at home but he had nothing to recall except her. His parents told him to get over his sluggishness and even tried to show him a way. "Life is all about plummeting and exalting. The other word for life is all kinds of ups and downs. Sometimes your spirits are on a pinnacle and sometimes down in the doldrums. When we become selfish, we get disturbed. However, we must know the basic trend of living and that is to confront life head on every single day. We are not allowed to leave it until we are off. Life only keeps on telling us where and how to move. Success, money, love, fame, feelings, dreams, status—these are transient things which go hand-in-hand and person-to-person and when your chance comes, you will get whatever you have dreamt of. Till that happens, just keep doing your *karma*. The main part of life is not to calculate, but to work and remember that if you have the power to dream, then your chances of getting something from these dreams will increase. So don't leave your work and forget all else that has happened."

"Son, you must have seen people trying to ameliorate all their failures; you must have seen people fighting for their rights; you must have seen people walking on different tracks in search of heaven and more. They do all this with their minds open. In case of love even, who gave you the right to feel hapless? In fact, you should strive to start a new life rather than going around with a long face. To me, love is nothing; it is just one more work to be done in twenty-four hours. Look at me, whether I go to office or not, in any case, I have to handle your mother. You should be happy as you have one lesser work to do at present."

"Listen, you just have to be true to yourself.
True life comes with lucrative desires,
true time never slips through fingers,
true relations never go insane, and
true feelings never remain hidden.
Enjoy the world by being true to yourself and to others."

Ayushman's father continued, "Life is too big, son and everything has a time-period. Things come and go. Ash is always found behind the smokescreen. There is a lot more which has to come yet, so you better start doing your work."

So he did learn a new lesson while at home. "Better to recollect everything," he thought. He stood up firmly and ramrod straight and the credit for this had to go to his parents. Ayushman returned to his school well before the scheduled time and this was in January 2005. He couldn't save himself from bouts of depression and often he wept on recalling his evil past, but he could now get a hold on himself. Even the principal of Scindia School couldn't believe that this was the same student who had shown such fervour and eagerness to work. Anyway, it was a relief to see him back at school. Now he was seen trying to get better every day rather than look like a lost person who had faced misery in life.

It is not easy to face the side effects of the disease known as love. Ayushman wondered how scientists had not discovered so far the antidote to suppress the effects of love and more so when it is one-sided.

I was hoping that he would do whatever he wanted. He now had a different mind on returning from home. "Previously I was doing my work for the nation so that they all could know about $E=mc^2$, but now I would like her to know what all I am capable of," he thought. At times, anger acts as a medicine to sloth and love." He felt somewhat motivated and pasted a quotation on his room's wall and of his lab too—'A feeling of anger never goes until it vanishes completely.'

He revealed his dedication and no mercy for his books. Basically 'hate' for the word 'love' was enough to make him go a few more miles. "Maybe I can do more work when I feel acrimonious," Ayushman told everyone who was helping him in his work.

Ayushman made it very clear that he should not be given any more holidays and he would be spending all his hours in the lab only. Despite facing many adversities in life, he could manage to recover himself and work with renewed energy to becoming a scientist.

"How did you manage to recover, Ayushman?" asked his friends.

"I would not have been able to face myself had I stopped simply because I had been ditched," Ayushman told them.

His pre-Boards started but for him it was like taking a nap on the table. He was yet to recover completely, but his present state was enough to handle the pressure. Everyone expected him to score the highest as he had done in Class X, yet some pessimists wondered, "Will he need a pacemaker to take him out from such a perilous condition?"

"Will it be possible for us to see him score the highest when they already know how downcast he is?"

"Would he be able to repeat history again?"

Scoring high marks was not the issue. For him it was necessary to show what a person can do with a healthy desire to become a scientist. Ayushman, however, didn't say anything or give a commitment to any college. It happened for the first time at Sicndia that almost every good college came up at the fort to pick him up. Scindia's top authorities and Deans of other colleges converged in the assembly hall to meet him. Colleges came with enticing promises to allure Ayushman but little did they know that he had already been enticed by someone who was most appealing for him. Therefore, there was nothing left for him to look at.

"I believe consistency and hard work are more important to do our work which is like a compendium too. I am good as long as I think like this. I just want to give everything what it takes to complete Einstein's experiment. I know you have gathered here on hearing about my qualities and are ready to do anything to take me in. It is easy for me to find that you have come here for $E=mc^2$."

"Please allow me to work more on it. Let me do what has never been done yet. Let me slog as others can never think of doing and let me live for $E=mc^2$ only. I am sure you would like me better when you find I have learnt more. If ever I think that I have grown enough or have become eligible to be a part of your family, then I myself would give you a call. With all due regrets I say that neither can I make any commitment nor should you ask me to give any justifications. Thank you all," he said to all the teachers and deans who came to the fort from different graduation-houses.

Only a few months were left for Ayushman to take his Board exam and also to submit the findings of his experiment to the higher authorities of the world. He had always wanted to be a scientist. His health was not good, he had lost his love, his friends were busy attending to their studies, but some of his teachers had high ambitions and expectations of him. Though feeling a bit lonely as everyone was busy in his own thing, he thought that perhaps I would take longer to complete my work. He asked the principal to give him more time in case he failed to complete the work within the stipulated time. Luckily enough, the principal agreed.

Ayushman felt that only if he could fall in love with $E=mc^2$ like he had fallen for Sneya, then he would succeed in his work. He began to devote more time and energy to his work. When you love your work, the work itself gives you whatever you want. You just have to feel it from within. The more you feel, the closer you reach. The closer you reach, the softer you feel. The softer you feel, the best you can get.

The dates for the Boards exam were put up on the notice-board and his preparations were going well within time. It was a great surprise for everyone to see Ayushman recover from such adverse conditions to emerge healthy and victorious. Just before the examination, Ayushman's friends said a one-minute prayer for Ayushman's welfare.

The Board exams were on and the students were in high spirits as though they had overcome their fears. A Scindian would normally feel fearless and dauntless, just because of a being a Scindian. Scindia School has a very hectic schedule which often makes a student fully capable of facing any difficulty. Everyone was about to leave the school as they were coming closer to completing their exams. So, they were more interested in sorting everything among each other.

Everyone was happily, joyfully and gleefully spending their last days of school-life as if it was the last time together. But their Boards were not over yet; a last paper, physical education, was yet to be tackled. In any case, it was apparently one of the easiest and scoring subjects in CBSE to date.

Ayushman's papers were almost over, except for the one on physical education. The format was simple enough for every student as 60 marks had been kept aside for the practical and 30 marks for theory. This kind of scheme made even the worst of the students take it easy. To score 60 per cent marks they just had to perform well in the field events and for the remaining 30 marks they had to study a book of less than 80 pages. The teachers were aware of this distribution and hence did not deem it necessary to pressurise the students to study.

The students hung around the campus, busy filling out diaries or slam-books—one of the oldest trends to say *Dusvidaniya* to friends. It is a well-known and most common way to say goodbye and it gives a good feel to everyone. There were about more than a hundred dairies floating everywhere at the fort with the juniors taking them across the houses. Some could be seen prowling with a dairy, a few with a piece of paper, still fewer with an oral message; some were on the hill and some were down the lane. At fort, as you are not provided any vehicle, you had to walk, walk, and only walk. Juniors acted as postmen, e-mail carriers, and couriers for their seniors.

The students wore a serious and dejected look as students from Class XII were about to leave and maybe to be seen never again. They were trying hard to be good to each other, but only a few of them succeeded in doing so. Some of them looked casual about it while a few preferred to remain tightlipped. In between all this, Ayushman too looked withdrawn about his dairy. He looked confused. "To whom can I send this?" he thought. Many names cropped up in his mind before settling down on the name, Anshul Agarwal.

He received the following letter from Anshul:

To dearest Ayushman,

Hello scientist! Firstly, I would not go into the details as I think a man like you doesn't need any kind of description. I can however say that among thousands of individuals, only a few come to occupy the place nearer to our hearts and that stock of friends or friend cannot be described in words. If I keep filling up the pages, even your persona would get lost. Secondly, I don't want to go from incident to incidents because I think that whatever we have done so far is not enough to be written like this on a limited surface.

I completely relished every moment that I spent with you, enjoying everything—moral or immoral. We started our sojourn from Dattaji house followed by Jayappa and then we drew closer with nothing there to make us drift apart. We matured with every passing year that we spent together. And I promise from the bottom of my heart that I truly appreciate your help in everything—personal or professional. But sometimes it happens that while leading our life we generally tend to forget what to wipe out and what not. We even forget to downsize our follies and foibles, so as to enhance our strengths.

Dude, you have much superior qualities and even then you concentrate on those who need your attention.

Now take a look at something unsaid:

- *Here I go, hello again! It may surprise you if I say that you are an extravagant shadow of all those supreme and less devastating powers which you put into unravelling the scientific world. It is good being a science-oriented person, but don't let your work become a victim of acrimony of others. Try to concentrate on others when needed or when they need you. In fact, it would help your reputation to get a boost socially, and would, indeed, make you friendlier.*
- *You are blessed with innumerable qualities which all of us should have had too in our kitties. I wish you to have more and more in your life.*
- *The final and the most indispensable point is that if someone understands you, then he or she would be able to distinguish between good and bad. I would like to say that you may not be able to use this for your own sake. However, people are often oblivious to the good they have within.*

I don't know what you would feel on reading this, but if you are looking for a morale booster, then read these three points till something gets awakened inside you. Really buddy, I was really very excited at writing this and felt very proud.

Initially, I was a bit worried about how to write, but as I started doing so, then every line made me feel better to write the next. I wish I would get more chances to write about you.

Love you
Anshul

Ayushman was very happy as he went through every line written in his diary. He found himself floating in the world of dreams and friends. We always need someone to hear us, to look at us, to support us, and Anshul provided all this, serving as a tonic for reviving one's sagging spirits. Later, all Class XII boys were invited to attend a farewell party given at the residence of the principal of Scindia School. It has been a trend since its inception and it is generally organised every year for the outgoing students of Class XII. As expected, all of them attended, making their presence felt in more ways than one. What is more, Ayushman too attended despite the work pressure. It was a party for the most talented batch of Scindia School of 2005. Every kind of arrangement had been made.

They were all welcomed as they entered the residence of the principal and found everything very decently done up; no pooh paah, no show, no pomp. The teachers were present in full strength and stood at the gate to receive them. Flowers were showered on them as though they were snowflakes dropping from the sky. Every heart was filled with emotions as they stood together for the last time and ready to go on their different paths. The principal moved along them, exchanging pleasantries with them. After a while, they all sat down on their respective chairs to enjoy the rest of the evening. After a while, they all stood up to sing the Scindian anthem for the last time together. This was followed by the screening of a short film on their victorious moments, their happiness, compassion, lively spirits, heart-rending speeches and the contribution made by each of them for their houses at the inter-house and inter-school levels. They all were moved to see their own presence on the Scindian screen and shared their feelings at leaving the school with each other. Every one of them agreed unanimously, "Scindian life can never be forgotten."

After this, they were all presented a memento by the principal himself. This ceremony took longer as the principal became a bit emotional when Ayushman came forward to receive his gift. The principal was not expected to give a speech commending Ayushman's contribution separately on such an occasion, but he could not control himself and said, "I have never seen such a talented student as Ayushman in my whole life. I have been in charge of running Scindia School since the past ten years but have not come across someone as impressive as him. He came here in 1998, yet he is as fresh as he was then. His energy level has not waned and he never took his work lightly. His potential, determination, honesty, skill—everything about him has rocked here. I think he alone could handle any work that needed group participation. I thank him for serving as a role model for others to emulate by those who follow him now. Thus, as an elder, I shower all my blessings on him and hope and pray that more like him will spring up when he has left this place."

Now it was the turn of Ayushman to speak as he had to return all the favours shown to him in school. He began: "I am grateful for all the help that has been forthcoming from all of you teachers and colleagues and in fact, whenever I close my eyes, I often see all of you applauding me. Now it's my turn to say a hearty thank you to all of you. It has been my good luck that every possible encouragement was given to me in whatever form I undertook. As the time draws near for me to leave the hallowed portals of the school, my throat chokes with emotions because I have spent some of the best days of my life here and this I can never forget. I have given plenty of speeches at Scindia and in every speech of mine I tried to portray a different Ayushman Agarwal. I wonder how much I have succeeded in this. My aim has always been to deliver as good as possible, so that no one would ever feel that I did not deserve the credit given by my teachers and the principal and that it was a favour shown to me."

"When I newly joined the Scindia, I said that I would try to be the best in my work while the school would do the rest for me. Now that I am leaving, I feel that Scindia did all that a mother does for her new infant. If I talk about it in general on behalf of everyone, then I can say that we already have taken lots of favours from Scindia and there is no way in which we can return them except for one and that is by becoming whatever Scindia has expected us to be. Every student here is great in his own way. Meeting any individual here is like going to a different planet as that is the way I felt. You automatically get what you deserve, provided you take steps to ensure that they do not fall into dirt or muck. The soil of Scindia is so potent that it pushes you forward till you reach somewhere."

"**Protectiveness:** As far as security is concerned, which is a very viable point when you join a new school, I firmly believe that being here was like being in heaven. I have never faced any threat. It was like being at home—leaving it when you wished and returning to it when you liked and going anywhere you desired; this feeling helped to boost our self-confidence and made us fearless. Sending a child to Scindia is like sending him to a secure world of education and entertainment."

"**Education system**: If I talk about studies, then I run short of words to describe the system. There are not enough words to describe the utility of the school's education system. The syllabi and school curriculum are so well planned that even those who have no aptitude for an activity learns to participate in it. Every student here is sublime and develops the capacity to grasp what is being taught. Education here is a complete entity in itself and provides for many options as per one's inherent capacity and interest. Every subject is unique and essential for the growth of a student; even the essence of it can make the student to acquire growth. Who can know better than me, who has been given every possible and impossible help in whatever form I have done and for what I have been trying for years. Scindia School has made me realise what it takes to be successful in your studies. I have even talked freely to the teachers who have been ever-willing to help and guide me whenever needed. My fellow students say that I am like a tall tree that gives them support and shelter, but what I would like to say is that whatever I am today is because of Scindia School. And my teachers have ever been very supportive and open not only when needed, but always. My teachers have taught me how to be successful and how to live a life with full passion. The education that is imparted here is exceptional as it helps in moulding you into a well-rounded personality. When you leave this school, then you will discover that the education given here is so good that you would come back here again and again. I am not boasting or expressing a biased opinion, but stating the truth as it is."

"Opportunities: At Scindia School, I have noticed that if you recognise yourself well, you can get hundreds of helping hands to your assistance. For instance, when I saw myself as a scientist, then all of you know what happened thereafter. Every one of you came to me. It happened because I had realised what I wanted. The same I would like you to do in your life. Truly, I am really obliged to see myself standing on the soil on which there stood luminaries like Yashwant Sinha, Dr A.P.J. Abdul Kalam, Shahrukh Khan who had come to boost us boys; it is the soil which may encourage you to become the next Einstein or Newton. What else are your dreams for?"

"Lastly, I just want to thank all the mighty and the lowly authorities of this school. I wish to thank everyone who has helped me, supported me, greeted me and loved me. I am happy to see that many others have come here as new teachers and as new students, and I wish all the older ones, who are going to retire, to lead a happy and contented retired life."

Everyone looked at him as though held spellbound by his rhetoric speech. He continued: "I just have a few more words to add to my fellow students. Everything can be gained, even when we feel not up to it. We should not waste a single minute of our life and soon we will realise that even twenty-four hours are not enough to complete our work. Hence, we must keep on at it if we want to go as far as we can. I wish best of luck to you all."

His speech left everyone stricken for a moment or two before they started buzzing like bees. His speech had connected with everyone's mind and said what others may have wanted to say also. On completing his speech, Ayushman was seen looking lost as though finding himself all alone in the midst of such a crowd. He went and stood in one corner till the function drew to a close. Even the glamour of the party failed to revive his spirits. Many of his friends tried to draw him out but he seemed to have withdrawn into his shell. He had other things on his mind, Sneya and her letter. The letter had robbed him of all his outspokenness and he felt like some mechanical robot doing what was expected of him.

Then came March 31, 2005. It was the day for the last paper and he gave his examination and came out quietly. It was his last Board exam and his expression revealed no feelings—no joy, no sorrow; it was a completely a pale face. He had not been able to erase the thoughts of Sneya from his mind. He was aware that both his professional and personal life were about to come to an end, with no substantive results to show. His Boards were over, his experiments were yet to be completed, and his love had got lost somewhere in the baneful world of humans and technology.

It also happened that students at SKV did not have to appear for the paper on physical education and so they had left the town before the Scindians could leave the fort. So before Ayushman could complete his Boards, Sneya had already left for home. He couldn't believe that it was not possible to see her in any manner whatsoever. This meant that he would never see her again and nor did she want to see him ever. Everything was over—his classes, his Boards, his life, his friends, his speeches, his fun. He had to stay back in school to complete the rest of his work while everyone else was packing to leave the fort and return home to join their college. It was I who told him to stay back as some more time was needed to complete $E=mc^2$, to give the final touches.

He got busy doing his work with me, while the others were seen frantically filling up forms for admission to different engineering colleges. Some of them feared that they would not get admission and may have to sit back at home for a year. Ayushman helped his friends to keep their luggage in the buses, while he himself felt tears springing up in the corners of his eyes. He was upset that it was his last official day with his friends. He was standing on the same field, the Madhav pavilion, from where he had joined his house on getting admission in Scindia. He watched his friends depart one by one when suddenly a letter was delivered to him by some unknown guy in school, though the writer was very close to him. He kept the letter in his pocket as he continued to see every Scindian leaving to start a new life at a new place. His friends came near to hug him and that made him feel good. One of them even commented. "You have a long way to go, Ayushman. Since you started your experiments, you have gone far from all of us. We don't even have any personal news about you any more."

"Okay, dude, can you give me a piece of paper so that we can exchange our contact numbers," said another friend of his. "As you are going to be a big person, I should have a mode of communication to send my congratulations to you later in life," he continued.

"Don't be so formal, dudes. I am not going to forget you guys at any point of time. Moreover, I will surely come across you all some day, once I complete my pending work here," said Ayushman.

As he didn't have any paper except that envelope which had been delivered to him and as he had no great interest in it, he handed over the same to his friend to note down the contact numbers. The other person took it and started writing on the front side of the envelope, when Ayushman suddenly noticed the name of the sender written over it. The boy completed writing his address and said goodbye to Ayushman. By the time the latter took the envelope back, the message in the envelope had been lost and only darkness could be seen. All his friends had left, buses had moved, houses had got empty, but Ayushman stood, looking at the name—Anamika Agarwal.

Confession

* * * * *

To Ayushaman

I feel so happy whenever I see you. All my feelings for you get unplugged and the heart beats fast too whenever I see you. I, indeed, lose my sanity whenever I see you.

But what you have felt in so many years I never got to know. However, things have changed and this letter is a witness of all that stuff. Every letter of each word, each word of each line, each line of each paragraph, and whole letter is true, but please try not to get this connection wrong. I know I will not be a part of your life after you complete reading this letter. Even then I will keep worshipping you as I did before—in whatever forms it demands.

This letter is covering all the unsaid and said things. I have enjoyed every moment with you, so it is not right to hide anything now. I have something to say which may seem strange to you but as any more delay will cause more ado, I am not in the mood to cheat you. I will behave the same way as I have done before, but maybe words can get you pissed off with me.

Some months back, we made a plan. Every one of us was included in the plan—a plan which was meant to betray you, to cheat you, to dupe you, but it was made with a good cause. It was a completely devastating plan which had been made to leave you alone in this world, so that you could come closer to me. We made it after your visit to SKV.

This letter includes two different shades for your consideration. There is a pure soul residing in you, so I would try not to fool you, but if I do, then my apologies. You might have come across this kind of style of writing earlier even and that is what you would find now too.

First, Ayushman, I love you and maybe this may make you angry or even generate a wave of vileness in you. But I have always liked you since you joined the senior school. It was like love at first sight. I fell in love with you when I saw you first in the class. I don't know which person will ever come in my life, but I will not stop loving you.

I think I am not needed to tell why and how this 'Love Story-2000' started in Class VII. It is similar to what you felt at SKV when you saw Sneya first. But unluckily none of us had a 'Kismat Konnection' with each other. I don't feel sorry for all this, but I do have a guilt that I've got late. I think I should have told you before you fell in love with Sneya, but I couldn't tell you exactly what I always felt for you. I strove many times to say 'I love you', but you didn't take it seriously. I even tried one day to express myself but at that time you gave your aim in life priority. So I had to keep shut.

At last I spoke to my Mom regarding all this but she told me to wait. As I had already done enough of waiting, I did what I wanted. I fell in love with you initially itself but had to wait for so many years to see when my love would turn into reality. However, when I found my love difficult to get, I made others to help me. I do not know whether I should have done this or not, but now there is no use to feel sorry, as I have already committed the biggest mistake.

<u>Second side of letter</u>

I, Mom (Anuradha ma'am) and Uncle (Arjun sir) belong to the same family as you know, and Anshul Agarwal too, as you don't know. Remember Anshul Agarwal, your best friend? He delivered your letter to her at SKV, isn't it? We were too young when our family broke off due to family differences, internal bickering and trials and travails among each other. Like every family, we too had disturbances, altercations, and confrontations. In fact, I have grown up seeing all this muck. In those days of anger, I was in a day-school.

Every day our parents fought, but unluckily that day it went out of control and turned violent, with never-ending accusations flung at each other. It all started when my mother, Anuradha Agarwal, found my father, Mr. 'X', had relations with a second woman. This came to her notice when my father started to go more than five times to Delhi every month as he had an office there. We were surprised when we got to know that he had a full family just as we were a family in Mumbai. Mom found all this during an enquiry done by her friends and this later became the reason for our separation. Anshul Agarwal is a son from the second and I wonder how I should address him.

Listen, don't get confused; let me clear more to you.

My mother and I shifted to Mom's mother's residence to live with her brother, Arjun sir. And we stayed there till we became financially independent. Then my mother took a couple of months to convince her brother to take things practically and my mother did not ask my father to give her any penny at the time of their divorce. I cleared my Class VI through home tuitions. By the time I cleared Class VI, my Mom had got a job here at Scindia. To be near my Mom, her brother came with her at Scindia and decided to work here too. We came here at fort to lead a free and independent life.

When we came here in 1999, then we got to know that Anshul had also joined Class VI at Scindia in 1998, a year before we came here. But we couldn't say anything to him as he had every right to study anywhere.

Why my father kept him in India when he already had lots of money, we don't know. We never asked. Why didn't he send him to some other place? We couldn't find out the reason—maybe to disturb us, or to influence us to accept him, or it was simply a coincidence. Mom was infuriated to find him here and told me not to go nearby. But it may surprise you that I took help from him only.

Ayushman, your letter was never sent to Sneha. You were always given a wrong picture. I told Anshul to do this for me as I had no other option. He did it to prove his brotherly love and I did this because I still love you. Anshul did this to improve his relations with us and I did this to improve mine with you. Anshul did this because he wanted us to live together as a family and I did this so that I could include one more member in our family.

Nobody was wrong as everyone had played their roles. But after doing this nothing good happened. We neither became one family as Mom told him to stay away from us, nor did you become mine as we are leaving today. Sorry to say it Ayusman, Sneya doesn't even know who Ayushman is or anything about your letter too.

I did not have any other way out. You always spent most of your time in the lab and the rest of your time in thinking about her, while I suffered and wept all the time. My aim was not to separate you from her but to bring you more close to me. Anshul is going to the States and perhaps he would pursue his graduation there only. I don't know about myself. I know this pinheaded decision of mine has let us down. Anshul ditched you, I cheated, you didn't get Sneya, I didn't get you, Anshul didn't get us back, and nothing happened as expected. We are so guilty that we both have decided that we will not meet you ever again.

Dude, there is only one thing left to do and this was started when we were all together. I request you not to leave your $E=mc^2$ as it is only one dream left among us. Do whatever you can for your experiment and give us a chance to be known as Einstein's friends of this century.

I hope you would produce some astonishing discovery to this world and I wish lots of prosperity and luck to fall at your feet.

From

Anamika

He had sent a letter to Anamika and thereafter her life came to an end. And after receiving her letter what did he feel? Sneya, whom he fell in love with, didn't know anything about him and Anamika, who had loved him, had left him to wallow in misery. On seeing this inhumane face of humans, he was left entirely on his own and he began to question himself where he had gone wrong? He thought whether it was the real face of humans which he had seen or was it more cruel than it had been? He began to feel the same sort of depression and stress he had felt when going through the Sneya phase. Earlier it was due to Sneya and this time it was due to Anamika Agarwal. In both cases, Ayushman had become the victim. He couldn't believe that Anamika could do this to him!

"Why did Anamika, Anshul, Sneya, Arjun sir and Anuradha ma'am do this with me?" His body stopped moving and he madly wanted to run away somewhere. He kept fiddling with the letter and debating in his mind what to do next. He could not focus his mind anywhere. "Whenever I tried to give myself an ambrosial touch, I was given a viscous blow at my heart," he thought. "Why? Is my heart a cuddly toy?"

But one thing, which was still a part of the picture, was his experiment—$E=mc^2$. His true source of inspiration forced him to get back to his work as it had done many times before too. If Ayushman had not this experiment to live for, then he surely would have died because of his pristine lifestyle. He was now left with $E=mc^2$ only.

However, it is often seen that when we have nothing to live for, then we start living for someone or something else. Ayushman wandered around the campus for some days as a tortured soul with a woozy looks across his face. He was trying to analyse the events in his life and piece them together but failed. In the end he could only tell himself, "Why blame others for all this?"

There was only one person now with him and that is me, Dr P. Smith. Since Class XII, he did not have a single close friend. He had no one except me. I was his superior/guide/friend/elder/companion/route-charter/explorer/doer. He had to live with me and believe me only. I thought, "I am pretty impressed by myself as I do know a person who believes in me. How would it feel when the next generation of Einstein only sees you, talks to you, follows you and obeys you? How would it feel when a person gets the least support from the world as if he were alone on the whole planet? What if you were to find a highly potent person bowing in front of you—should it make you laugh or cry at his condition? What should a person feel when he realises that soon he may get what he has always wanted?"

Ayushman was completely dejected and crestfallen. I realised his sorrow alone would open every door for me to make him my best friend and confidant. "One has to lay a trap and wait till the other person shows emotions; that is the time to hit him because he is in no condition to retaliate," I thought while we had coffee together. Ayushman was engrossed in discussing everything with me, so that I would provide him some solace. But I had different plans for him and every sip of my coffee was making me feel more and more victorious as he kept revealing every aspect of his life. I got so hyper that I started recalling the day when I had a cup of coffee with the principal during my interview that was held in 2004. I had joined Scindia to use him, so that he could complete my dream—the dream to derive $E=mc^2$. It was my dream too and I knew I couldn't complete it during my heydays. This was the only thing which I couldn't do in the UK, despite possessing ample resources. I did not have the brain that Ayushman had and which was needed to derive $E=mc^2$.

When I saw I was not reaching anywhere, I decided to try my luck back home in India. When Scindia sent me the invitation to join the faculty, I jumped at the opportunity as I had learnt from them about Ayushman. It helped me regain my energy for work. But Ayushman was always unaware about the crooked intentions I had been harbouring since my days in the UK. He was verifying his experiment by studying it from every possible angle while I eagerly awaited the completion of his work. I told him to work diligently and like an obedient student, he kept himself confined to his lab as if he were locked in his cell from which he was not allowed to escape.

"Where life is concerned, things happen which one has to face. No one can run away or hide; you just have to confront them." Thus Ayushman motivated himself. He had already progressed far ahead in his work and discovered new theories to substantiate his findings despite feeling intense loneliness.

There was no subject left which he hadn't studied thoroughly. He had almost completed his work but it was yet to be handed over to the higher authorities in the world. As he was giving the finishing touches, he kept himself away from every possible distraction. The date of becoming another Einstein was drawing near and he had to expedite his work. He was waiting for the day and date to appear when he could do what he had always wanted. He then increased his speed.

As he was all alone at Scindia, every teacher would stop by to talk with him. When everyone had left him alone to bear his pain, it was the teachers who were his only companions. They tried to make him feel at home.

Anshul had left for the States for his graduation.

Anamika had already passed out from school.

Sneya, where was she? Did she know anything?

Arjun sir and Anuradha ma'am too had left and gone somewhere. No one knew where they had gone.

Only Ayushman was left standing at the same base from where he had started a few years ago—a picture of desolation, forsaken and rejection by the world. He was intensely lonely in the school with no one to call his own, except his father's footprints. For him days held no direction; sleep robbed him of dreams; the mind was left with no healthy plans; the heart was left with no heartbeats and life was left with no breath. He was left with no choice; otherwise he surely would have dropped the idea of being a scientist too. He even had decided not to continue once he were to finish his pending work. He wanted to go off somewhere forever. He was alone, yet dedicated towards his work. His life was still moving as if he had been loaned his time by the Almighty. His teachers used to come in his lab to visit him and whenever they saw him doing his work, they invariably remarked, "From now on, Ayushman will always move ahead and leave this world behind to remember his work."

Unfortunately, I was standing next to him when they were saying all this rubbish. "It is a common fact that no one knows about one's future. How can his teachers ever be soothsayers to be able to predict what will happen next?" I thought. "When I am here, then how can anyone expect good to come in his life? No one can help him; no one can predict his future; no one can support him and nothing will happen right in his life since I am his fate-maker. I won't allow time to give him anything until I want it so."

A professor had got him to work as his slave, but Ayushman had no one who could do anything to console his heart, though his friends had taken a piece of it for their respective uses.

"Is there still someone behind the façade who can hurt him now?" I may ask.

"Of course, I am here." If I hadn't entered the lab with a selfish motto, then his story of being a scientist would have been different. I am sorry to tell the readers that I did something cruel, as I had no other way to prove myself a great sucker. I know my act was downright mean, but I was there at Scindia for $E=mc^2$ only and I had to do it anyway. I was completely tired of being his master always and had become weak by prowling here and there for him. I felt I too had put in a lot of hard work in it, so I deserved to be the master of $E=mc^2$. I had spent so many years of my life abroad trying to solve the puzzle. I took help from books, used existing and pre-existing technologies, worked on latest machineries, spent a lot of hours in labs with top-notch scientists of the world, but I couldn't make it anyhow. I was always considered best in my field but my skilled and honed attempts came to a naught whenever I tried to derive the formula. I always managed to countermand every possible obstacle coming across, yet I couldn't solve the puzzling riddle $E=mc^2$ ever. And luckily now I had a chance here at Scindia to complete my work, to realise my dreams and therefore I had said 'yes' to all of them. If it were not for $E=mc^2$, I surely would have said 'no' to them. It was $E=mc^2$ which had officially brought me here; not the seductive salary they had offered to me at my interview. Now it was time to recover what all I had given to him and to his work. Therefore, I took an imprudent decision which struck him to the bone and he nearly lost his mind. Take a look at what it was.

A Bolt from the Blue

* * * * *

I entered his lab with a scheme in my mind. I didn't give him a warm hug as it would have surprised him. Teachers are always expected to respect their students, but I didn't do it. Moreover, I was less sedate and more bestial to him. He was asking me to sit, to drink, to eat, and I? I stood there, making abrasive remarks about his simplicity. "Good and bad, both are part of life and a person should learn to accept both of these," I said to him. Instead of wishing good day, I made a sarcastic comment, though I could not help but think, "It is not a good start at all." My comments as well as expression were intriguing him.

"I cannot understand you, sir," he said in a resigned voice as he had been working since the morning. Since he knew nothing, he could only utter only one thing.

"What? You have done so well in your experiment but it is very difficult for someone to believe what you have done. So, I am here to set you free forever, Ayushman. I am here to extricate you from your trouble and misery."

"Sir, I have always given top priority to my project, then how can I be tired of my own work?" Ayushman asked.

He was completely unaware of what was going on in my mind and was wondering what I meant when I said 'set you free'.

"There is no question of getting tired, sir," he repeated.

"Good, but your realm of $E=mc^2$ will not be able to make you a scientist."

"Why?" he asked in a confused tone.

"No one would ever believe that an austere student from Class XII could have derived $E=mc^2$ in his life."

Now Ayushman was getting some idea about my cruel intentions. He stopped smiling and his expression looked as though he had been hit by a rock. "What exactly are you trying to convey, sir?" he asked in a bewildered tone.

"Listen, your theory should be given the respect that it deserves."

"How?" he asked.

"Ayushman, now your part is over and allow me to become you," I said. I added, "If you want your work to be globally accepted and recognised, then give it to me officially by my name," I suggested brazenly. "See, you haven't yet completed Class XII nor do you hold any degree. It would be futile on your part to think that you are the only brilliant scientist in this whole world."

It was a lethal blow that I delivered through my words. He understood each and every word I had uttered and replied weakly, "Sir, unfortunately, you are among those who have ditched me in my life." He looked extremely upset and tears welled into his eyes.

"I know," I replied. As I knew that I was cheating him, I could not say anything more.

"How can you be so audacious when you know all this is my own hard-earned labour?"

"It is not your hard work. However, you have merely used what you have possessed in large amount and that is your inherent skills with which you are blessed in ample measure."

"Whatever may be the fact, this all belongs to me."

"Nonsense, it was all an easy task for you to do," I said, as if to downsize him. I was trying to show that it all entailed a small amount of work and not as much as he professed.

He could not utter a word and he looked as though he had lost his voice. He was drained of all colour as if he had lost all his sanity, gaiety and integrity in a minute. He just couldn't believe how his own professor could ever behave thus with him. In a very meek, dismayed tone he muttered, "Can you please leave now?" He began closing the windows and doors of the lab. Perhaps he feared me as he walked back to his hostel. He was very tense and took nearly a thousand rounds of his room to decide what he could next. Tears kept streaming down his eyes, his breath was coming in gasps, the veins in his forehead were swollen and beating fast as if they would burst any moment. While taking his rounds, he kept on cursing himself. He started recalling everything, every day, every night, every session, every theory, his lab, and his $E=mc^2$ which he had shared with me. He was computing what all I knew about him and trying to think if anything at all had been left which I didn't know about his work. But, as always, he had no answer and had no one to provide the answer either. He wanted to talk about this to someone, but he didn't as he had to protect the image of his professor, that is, me. He kept himself confined to his room. He would not have gone to anyone even if I had tried to kill him, in fact. He was more keen to wind up things rather than reporting the matter to the higher authorities in the school. His experiment was almost over and he just wanted to give it a last glance, a last revision to cover up all the loopholes that may have remained. The feeling of being hunted kept him awake for hours on end in his room. A few days later he would have been declared the king of science and the youngest scientist. The day he was eagerly looking forward to was nowhere to be seen even in his dreams. He was trying to find ways of keeping me off the work he had done. He had to be ready for every eventuality and he kept thinking, mumbling and walking. Since all kinds of horrendous thoughts plagued his mind, he couldn't sleep till 1:30 a.m., 2:15 a.m., 3:45 a.m., as time kept slipping past. Only a few more hours were left for the next day to begin when he could have changed history. He felt extremely fatigued due to excessive thinking. He stood next to his bed, thought for a couple of minutes and leaned slightly towards his pillow. He then lowered himself on his bed and kept his head on the pillow. He closed his eyelids to ease his mind before he slowly dozed off to sleep. He was so tired that he didn't even change his clothes, didn't take his shoes off and didn't remove his books from his bed. He just kept lying on his bed till the local authorities came next morning to wake him up at 9 a.m.

July 31, 2005 was the day which was witness to premedintated plans, unscrupulous behaviour and downright cruel attitude.

Next day, Ayushman went to his lab as he did on any other day, but he behaved very strangely this time. He seemed to be searching frantically for something. He quickly got down to his work and glanced at his labour of love. He still had all those points alive in his mind which he had gone through the previous night. He was in no mood to waste even a second and continued doing his work. Suddenly he saw me in his lab again and withdrew a few steps automatically as if he had seen a ghost. His face exuded fear, sweat rolled down from every pore of his body, his eyes blinked rapidly and he looked shocked. He soon recovered from the effect of seeing me and said, "I told you not to come here."

"I am here to say sorry," I said.

"Your sorry will not pacify me, sir."

"I won't disturb you any more because I am leaving today."

"Good. Now, what do you want me to do? Hug you?" asked Ayushman ironically.

"I want nothing; I only want to see you keep working."

"I have heard this a number of times earlier too. People, in some way, come in my life, show affection to me and then treat me like a plaything. If they win, it is okay, but if they lose, then they leave the place with the message 'keep going' and this is what you have done just now. Can you tell me, sir, how many times do I need to revive myself because of your insane acts? Is it possible for you to compute how many times have I been menaced? It is always easier for someone to do something wrong with someone, but it is always tough for the person concerned to handle the after effects of the assassin. Go away from here, sir," he said, as if drained of all energy. He showed no compassion for me either. "Leave," he said in a commanding tone.

On seeing his anger which I had never seen before, I took leave from there and left the lab in a jiffy. "What does he think of himself? Does he think he is free now? Perhaps not," I said, while coming downstairs. In some way, I was not planning to leave. I just wanted to ease his mind so that he could complete the work in peace without my evil shadow stalking him. "I know my mind and I am not going to leave him until I have completed my job."

I was busy planning the future course of my action while he was left with no solution. He continued doing his work with a lost smile. He could no longer concentrate as much as he wanted and all the worst moments of his life kept coming to his mind again and again. He seemed to have lost all control over his senses and often felt that he was seeing me around him everywhere as if he were hallucinating.

Crime is committed when the sun has set to make someone wait impatiently to get into his act. It was rather late; later than it was expected. He was working in his lab and fighting the shadows of his life. As usual, he was working there alone. Arjun sir had already left with Anamika. He had no energy left; his fingers even couldn't wobble on the table; his vision had blurred and it seemed as if his heart had stopped to palpitate. However, he fell on his table, feeling giddy.

In life there is always a black shadow present to prevent a conscientious person from doing his work. Remember, here I am referring to myself. Possibly this may be the last betrayal in his life to suffer. In return for his hard work, he was going to be presented a return-gift on that night by me. I was waiting impatiently slightly away from his lab.

I had been waiting for him to fall asleep. But why I had forgotten all my duties I don't know. All I knew was to win glory, be it by hook or by crook. After all, this was a question of life and death for me and would change my life forever. As he slept, I had to decamp with all his hard-earned labour. I entered his lab very comfortably but couldn't find the box lying nearby. I stumbled and fell on to the floor, though I had been very careful to ensure that I did not make any noise. Ayushman quickly stood up from his cushioned seat as he caught my desultory attempt to steal his work on $E=mc^2$.

"Can I ask you the reason for your presence here, sir?" he asked. "I remember you telling me that you were leaving, but it seems you are not." He had sure enough noticed the greed shining through my eyes and evil writ large on my face. He said nothing to me and darted out of the lab with unbelievable speed, carrying all his indispensable work with him. As it was his project, he knew very well what he was supposed to pick and run. He had kept everything aside, except for a few pages which provided vital information for the experiment.

As it was too late for him to go to any teacher for help, he ran straight out into the dark.

He had to be fast and so was I.

His action was far from impressive but it was taken on the spur of the moment to save his experiment and run. He went darting, searching for a safe haven while I tailed straight behind him. Outside the lab, along the roads, between the passages, we ran past the local, dark, less-populated area. I had to catch him as he was with something important, while he had to run fast as the papers belonged only to him. As it was pitch dark, no one saw us running. Both of us were running madly, with one looking for help and the second for catching the one looking for help. I ran so fast that I succeeded in landing some hard blows on his back so as to stop him on his running feet. However, this ugly act of mine failed to deter him from running.

I, who showed Ayushman the way to establish himself as a scientist, was now hell bent on snatching Ayushman's experiment and Ayushman, who had always done everything to succeed as a scientist, was trying his level best to save it from my clutches. We reached somewhere in a dark, forested area where even we could hardly see each other, but our running continued, seeming like an endless chase. We were running and going through the paces where none of us had ever been before. Basically, I was chasing his footsteps; not him. But, after a while, I noticed that the footsteps which I was chasing had suddenly stopped and there was no sound anywhere. I halted, trying to locate him, but there was no sign of him. He seemed to have disappeared into thin air, or entered the earth's womb, or maybe just vanished from the scene.

"But, where could he have gone?" I thought. Unbelievable! I just couldn't believe my eyes. The place was empty, and I gave up dejectedly. I didn't try to go any further. I thought of returning to his lab, hoping to discover something related to the experiment that Ayushman may have forgotten and left behind. I started walking back towards his lab with laboured steps, while thinking about him. "If only I had been a bit more careful, then maybe he could not have escaped from me," I said to myself. It was completely outrageous on my part to lose him. By this time I had reached the lab and was simply on the point of imploding.

I caught sight of flames leaping out of the lab and soon it was engulfed in tongues of fire, with reasons for the fire unknown to everyone. That guy had spent hours ensconced in the lab and now he and his lab had come to an end with no healthy reason for it. It lay burning in front of my eyes and I found myself helpless to do anything about it. My wait of long years and my ambitions were all blown away by the wind that was blowing the flames still higher. I had never ever seen such a raging fire in my whole life. Flames of the fire were slowly and slowly engulfing all the surroundings into its bosom. I stood there, watching dejectedly with nothing in my hands—neither Ayushman nor his work.

"Why did I do this? What have I got now?" I thought as I felt guilty at the way Ayushman's life had ended.

My thoughts went to the past and I recalled everything about Ayushman's life and cursed my own sins. "A middle-class family boy (Ayushman) had left his home and his parents behind to come to Gwalior and achieve something. In the end he perished with no denouement just because of me," I thought. "Ayushman had forsaken everything for his work and now even his hopes lay dashed to the ground because of me. I killed him, killed his life, killed his dreams and killed his desire of becoming an Einstein. It all happened due to my greed which drove him to take this extreme step."

The same day I woke up from a long, deep slumber, realising my mistake, but it was too late to repent for I had already killed him. "Nothing can be changed now." By the time I could come to my senses, everything was all over. "I just wanted his work; but instead I took his life," I lamented.

His lab was reduced to ash and every bit of labour had become dust. I could see only dark smoke billowing in the sky which was so dark that it seemed covered with soot. I kept standing at one spot, carved into a statue till the others arrived. And as they came, everyone stood rooted to the spot. I was totally stressed out by now. My throat felt choked due to the horrific act that I had committed. "Everyone is looking for Ayushman, but he has left no footprints behind him," I thought on seeing the others.

The fire had drawn everyone out—the principal from his residence; the housemasters from their houses; the servants from their quarters and even the empty barracks stood witness to the macabre sight at the fort. The searing fire had not only razed the lab, but tonnes of hopes and aspirations to ash.

"A revolution would not come now and neither would he," mumbled a voice. "Where is Ayushman?" was the question on everyone's lips, fearing the worst. They had lost the most desirable and loved one at the fort.

"Has he got burnt or has he run away somewhere?" asked a bystander while discussing with others.

"How could it have happened?" was the unanimous question and no one knew the answer. Everyone stood speechless with downcast faces.

I was the only person who knew everything, but I kept my trap shut.

All of them tried to douse the fire but failed. The fire had blown away everything—even the last shreds of the lab. Every possible route to meet or see Ayushman was closed forever now.

Even the moon could not find any signs of Ayushman's presence and the black smoke had obliterated his dreams of becoming what he had always wanted. Everyone was in tears as they had lost someone special to them—the teachers had lost their favourite student, the housemaster his best house-boy, the students had lost their role-model, the friends had lost the most helpful pal, and the whole school had lost their Einstein.

Anamika had lost a person whom she had loved the most, but she didn't know anything about his sudden demise as she had already left for some unknown place after her Board exams with her family. Senya had lost a person who had loved her the most, but she didn't know anything as yet.

"What a tragic blow I have given to them," I thought.

This story with a few main characters—Ayushman, Sneya, Anamika, Anshul and Dr Smith—who were all close to each other and had worked in unison for years and now, in the end, no one knew anything about anyone.

No one knew who loved whom and why.

No one knew who went where and why.

No one knew who died and who survived.

No one knew the reasons behind the strange happenings which had occurred in their lives.

Where he was no one knew. 'Was he alive or not?' no one knew.

But what we do know is that Ayushman had at last discovered *who was what to whom.*

Tryst with the Unknown

* * * * *

I have told you many things about the calamities which befell him, but one question might come to your mind and that is how do I know all this?

What do you think? Who am I, this Prof. Paul Smith? I am someone else. I am unknown. The professor was just the narrator of this story and I am a writer who has culled all aspects of Ayushman's life since his school days to weave this web. If I knew what had happened with him when he was a kid, then I too would not have been much older than him. Of course, I was a kid only—a kid who had lived with him, a kid who had seen him grow and a kid who knew everything since the time of his birth.

So, there is one more thing left which needs to be revealed. That is, I too belonged to Scindia. Basically, I had my bed next to Ayushman's in Dattaji house. I too was allotted to Jayappa house with him, though I never told you this. I was completely horrible in everything and couldn't do justice with those who were responsible for my birth. I was a kind of thug in my heydays. I was notorious for all my dare—devilry acts which I indulged in with boys. I was considered a trouble-maker by students and therefore was often kept locked in some kind of a store-room for days as if I were responsible for 29/11. When I was in Dattaji, I used to wake up by 5 in the morning so that I could roam around the house for hours with my tea-mug. I used to do this so that I could disturb the sleeping tigers of my house. I used to roll down their pants, hide their clothes to make them late for school, add water in their oil bottles, and when they came for a bath, half asleep and half awake, offer them mosquito-repellent cream instead of Colgate. However, my morning activities only helped me to meet the boy whom you know as Ayushman.

I had several things to do in the morning—take a bath, attend to my unpalatable activities and watch Ayushman work with his friend Anshul. Had my parents seen them study so conscientiously, they surely would have killed me. Both these boys, Ayushman and Anshul were Agarwals and completely wedded to their studies. Both of them were 'bed partners' as the junior school had 'bunk-beds.'

Now let me introduce myself—I am Bharat Agarwal. I was next to them. From that time till now I have been a fan of Ayushman. He was hardworking, outspoken, lively, supporter, cheerful and ever-ready to work for everyone as if he was an 'Eveready' battery. Their morning studies and my morning activities ran parallel to each other. Ayushman had often told me not to indulge in my activities, but I didn't pay attention to him in the beginning. As the school is at the fort, it used to remain cool during the summers even. Therefore, the boys would be slow in leaving the warmth of their blankets and Anshul too was one of them. Ayushman however got up on time and was never affected by anything.

To me there was hardly any difference between Ayushman and Anshul till I found the latter had ditched Ayushman. They were very close but differences arose between the two. Due to the same timings, we started cuddling each other and got to know each other very well. I kept passing my time by watching both of them and they kept passing their time reading something pleasant. By now, we were good friends. I was completely fascinated on seeing Ayushman as a student. I drew close to him as a friend but the way he led his life left me more amused. "How can someone be so singular-minded?"

He was complicated to understand as if he were not human. His work was very tedious and he seemed a bit crazy because of his devotion to studies. Whenever I saw him, I wondered what he might be thinking about me—a hoodlum perhaps! I didn't know. I didn't care. But for me he was the hero of the century. One morning, I was taking a bath. It was not like any other shower which I had taken earlier in the same bathroom. It was something different that day—maybe it was an 'awakening' shower for me. I entered the bathroom with Italian marble cold beneath my feet. I took off my clothes and stood in the nude. I started shivering. Before I could start, I just made some adjustments. First, I dragged one chair from my room and kept my soap, shampoo, conditioner, shower-gel, and body oil on it as if I were shooting for some kind of a bathroom commercial. Second, I opened the front window to get a clear view of the dancing sky above my head. Third, I checked whether the ventilators and fans were working. Fourth, I switched off the lights to save some electricity. Fifth and most important one, I cleaned all the mirrors around me so that I could see my bare body while bathing. And then finally I set some other minor things which were around me. Soon, I was under the shower and water came streaming down on me in rivulets. As the water was a bit cold and was spurting at a fast speed, I was enjoying my shower when I saw him enter the bathroom to give himself a last touch—settle his hair and to his dress, before leaving for class.

"What is he meant for?"

"How was he born?"

"Why did he come to Scindia?

"Could Scindia ever gratify his needs?"

"Why has he been chosen to do this much?"

"Is he normal?"

"Is he good in everything he does?"

These were the thoughts that assailed my mind. "Why should I bother? Who am I to know what all he has?" the questions continued. I don't know what happened to me when I saw him, but Ayushman left a vivid picture on my mind. "Who will provide the answer? Of course, someone should be there on this planet," thought I, while taking my bath. "Where can I start from?"

Ayushman stood for a moment or two and left, leaving me to cogitate further over his inborn skills. "Neither can I guide him nor can I ask for his help. I am just a tenderfoot in front of him. But I truly feel he would do wonders unless someone assassinates him. But suppose he does well in life, then would anyone be there to tell about him to the world? If he doesn't, then again would anyone be there to tell the same?" I thought, as if he were going to be the youth icon. "His life is busier than usual and he is not so good with his social pyramids. He has no fun. He keeps sitting next to his books. He never goes to any place except his classroom. He has nothing in mind except his own dreams, but who will take care of all this? Why don't I do something? But what can I do for him when I know I am not so good? Then what am I good at? Is there any way through which I can help him?" Such thoughts kept bothering my mind.

"Through sports? No."

"Through studies? No."

"Then physically? No."

"Mentally? No."

"What is left then?"

"Is there anything there to make it possible?"

"Through writing. Yes, it is a way out. It is only a way I have at the moment," I thought and decided to write something on him. "Normally I am free, but now I will get something to do. I will write about every phase of his life without culling anything. I will give birth to the writer in me so that I can do justice with his life decorously while doing my writing. My story will coerce others to read about him. I will try to include every minute, every class, every one of his projects, his junior life, his senior life, his papers, his friends, his critics, his awards, his speeches, his teachers, his love, his family and Scindia School. I hope I can complete it on time," I thought while taking the shower.

I began to follow him everywhere, even at the cost of my studies. In any case, there are always many advantages in having a godfather. "And I am not only doing it for him. If I could write well, then maybe it will help me earn fame in the literary world," thought I.

I tried capturing his every minute, but due to his hectic schedule, many a time I missed him. In fact, after a while, I told him everything that I thought about him. He was only too glad to find a person who was keen enough to write about him. Now we had a potent combination of a scientist and writer walking together. One was doing twisted things and the other was writing it down simply. But Ayushman told me to balance all the sections. He told me not to highlight his scientific world but write a story based on boarding life and in the end it had to be a masterpiece. He told me to start from the beginning when he joined school and I did exactly the same. We both started on this non-credit-based project, keeping it untitled till a suitable time came. "As the story is running with us, it won't be a good move to decide the topic so soon. Just keep going and we will decide on it, once it is completed," he said to me.

Ayushman allowed me to accompany him wherever he went—to school, to house, to meetings, and to many other places which we had in school. He didn't have any fear of anything, maybe because he was being written about. He used to share everything with me and guide me through the process. He, in fact, told me about other writers so that I could learn from their work. We started to stay together for long. He encouraged me at every step, so much so that I started enjoying writing on him. As I wrote something, he allowed me to see him at his workplaces. His preparation room, his studies, shouts of encouragement for his house, meetings with superiors, high spirits at sport meets—everything was on my list. Sometimes Ayushman himself came to me with some piece of sizzling news so that I could append that too.

"Ayushman is learning from his teachers, teaching his friends, helping his housemaster, studying with Anshul, guiding Anamika, working in the lab with Smith, writing with me. What else can one do?" I thought. I was his mobile diary, who stayed close behind him. But there were places where I was not allowed to go with him—his car and his lab were out of bounds for me. Therefore, we used to share his lab and car moments at night before we went to sleep.

No one else was allowed to do the same. We took our task very seriously and secretively that no one in the hostel had a hunch about it. My story improved with every passing day. I recorded all his good work and sinister shadows of his life at one point. He told me how he had fallen for Sneya at SKV, how Anamika had spoilt his life and made her own life a mess so as to ensnare him, how

Dr Smith entered into his life and how life took turns thereafter.

I was told to pen down everything without showing any emotion. Ayushman told me to be neutral—neither 'for' nor 'against', but the day he told me about Prof. Smith and about his wishful thinking, I lost all my coolness and became angry. On 30th, he came with a nervous look and fretful expression on his face. On asking, he went into all the details, telling me his story till he fell asleep.

July 31, 2005.

He went to his lab as he was plagued by some haunting fear in his mind. He couldn't tell about this to anybody. As that was the last day of his with me, we met for the last time. He would have been saved had I stopped him from going to his lab. I was in the guest house as I had to complete his story.

I was simply unaware of what had happened till I noticed the flames and then I saw people trying to quench the fire. I quickly went to the spot and witnessed the scene myself. I couldn't find Ayushman anywhere and everyone was feeling sorry for him. But none could find the root cause for the incident. Everyone stood silent with no idea of anything. They were blank as if they had just started their lives. What should be done was all that they had on their mind. I was standing very close to his lab as if I were trying to locate him inside. I felt depressed.

"I have lost someone who was my main lead, a true inspiration and a path-finder," I thought. I was recalling every day of our life together and all those moments shared till that merciless incident happened. I was worried about my writing and what would be its state now. Perhaps both the things (Ayushman and his story) were demented as they had lost their respective ends. I was standing next to the lab. If I had gone a bit closer, then it would have been my last day too. I was crying and hoping in my heart to find him somewhere. On my way, I found another person who was sober like me. As I stepped forward I discovered who he was.

"Hi, professor," I said in greeting. His pair of spectacles was dangling on his face, his hair was grey, face shaven, shirt neatly tugged in, trousers properly fitted, shoes matching his clothes. Who else could it be? Yeah, he was the villain of my book. "Perhaps I got someone who would help me to reach to the end of my story," I thought. I felt relieved that I had found the right person who I presumed to have been dead in this accident. I drew closer to him.

"Who is he?" he asked me. I heard his voice for the very first time in my life. He looked very simple and suave as if he didn't know anything; as if he didn't do anything.

"Bharat Agarwal, don't worry. I won't cause you any hurt, sir. Just tell me clearly what happened here," I said as he was the only person left to be questioned.

"How do I know?" he said as if he had been born a day before. "I came here just as you are here."

"Professor, come out clean and don't dilly-dally. I know about you, about Anuradha ma'am, Arjun sir,

Anamika, Anshul, Sneya and about $E=mc^2$ as well. I know everything, sir."

"So, what can I do in this? This is something which everyone knows by being in the same school. He was an icon here, so most of us know about him. Listen! I just lost my student, so allow me to remember him for the time being. It would be very kind of you to leave me alone for a while." He went and stood at another spot which was about a few metres away from me. I simply followed him with a sober smile on my face.

"What do you want from me?" he asked with impatience.

"I simply don't want you, sir. I just want the bloody information."

"What information?"

"Professor, I confess that what I told you about Ayushman will not satisfy you. But then how am I to know what all happened on the last day in the lab?" I said.

"What?" he asked, as if to find out what I knew about him.

"I know that you had approached him for his work and your overpowering greed simply eradicated him and his work from this world."

"What do you want?" he asked, as I saw guilt written on his face.

"I just want to know what all happened here."

"What will you get from this?"

"I am his writer. Therefore, I am the most deserving candidate to know all this."

"How is it possible?" the professor asked because he could not believe that a student could be a writer for his own batch-mate.

"Sir, how could a teacher behave like a devil for his own student?" I asked. "And, above all, he was not like those who are born every day, sir." I then explained to him everything as to how we had met and how he would share his work with me all along. "I just want to complete this book as I am looking for a plausible end," I said. "If I can complete it, then maybe I can repay his love which he had given me."

The professor inhaled deeply as he found it all completely indigestible. He wondered how he couldn't get someone like me to write about his life instead!

Then we sat together for rest of the day. It was 31st and a day later, on August 1, 2005, we were to have a new generation of students at Scindia, so we decided to be quick. He was free as he had lost his student and I was free because I had lost a person on whom I was writing. We were left with no one; we only had each other's companionship. He started very slowly and came out with every minute detail which I never knew. He revealed everything that had happened with them. Somewhere he knew that it was the only way by which he could pay back for his sin. We both tried giving a final shape to the story. We had to amend many details and finally we compiled everything. We expanded the major sections which were more important and cut down the weaker ones. We did the final editing before we were ready with the story of the indomitable boy and his never-ending dream—the dream to be the topmost in science, to become the next Einstein and earn fame. Unfortunately, he didn't get anything except a bit of appreciation all along his school life and now we were giving his life back to him through the story. Now Ayushman will live his life again via his own story. This time he will get what he always deserved—his fame. From now on Ayushman will be immortal as words never die.

Words neither die nor do they fade away. They live for centuries for the posterity to read.

Suddenly, the next instance, the professor stood up and started walking away from me. "Sir, where are you going?" I rushed after him as we were not done yet.

"My job is over and I have no courage left to stay here any more, son. Don't worry, son, we have already set everything, haven't we?" he asked politely of me.

"What about the first chapter, sir?" I asked as I was worried about him.

"Yes! I would come back to the same land, but I would come here when I find this book in the hands of your readers," he said as if he had decided on some final role for himself.

"Why?"

"Don't you know why I am doing this?" the professor asked.

"Are you paying back to him like this, sir? This is insanity, sir," I shouted at him as if I were years older than him.

"No matter what you say, it has to be done like this. Now your readers will decide my fate," the professor said.

"And what will you do till I complete the publication part?" I asked him curiously.

"I will prepare myself to die," he said as if he was preparing to receive the gold medal for his stupidity. "In fact, I would be among those who would know when they would die."

"Why?" I urged him.

"I had killed his dreams. What else do I deserve? I have to end myself at the same place where I started. I will perish here only so that I can find his soul."

"Okay, can you tell me the title and name of the author?" I asked as I had to finish my book anyhow.

"I am fraught with sins, so my name as an author would not go down well with it, though I would prefer to be the narrator. You had done nice work too and you were closer to him. So why don't you want to be the author?"

"What would be the title then?" I asked since he had more experience than me.

"The author should decide this; not the narrator," he ended.

He walked away from me and I didn't want to keep Ayushman's story a secret any longer like some hidden treasure. I could have given my script for publication earlier even, but I was giving more time to Prof. Smith. First, it was an indirect way to give him time to repent over his blasphemous act to be Ayushman. Second, it was a way to give him more time to live. Ayushman had got lost somewhere and he had left, giving others a chance to be Einstein. He was born to find the mysterious derivation of $E=mc^2$ but by the end, he had himself become an unbeatable mystery.

"If you do something, then do it until you last. Do it like never before and try to make it charismatic too." Ayushman used to tell me this and I am truly glad that I could complete his book the way he had wanted.

Next day I went to attend the 'last words' for Ayushman spoken by the principal of Scindia School.

When I had joined Scindia, I had attended the unforgettable orientation session given by the principal and where Ayushman made the memorable speech and now when I was leaving, I had to attend his funeral.

"We are here to pay tribute to that person who has changed our very approach towards science. He showed us a new path, gave us a chance to rethink about ourselves and helped us get a glimpse of Einstein's work. Long queues were always found in front of his house and outside the assembly hall to catch a glimpse of him. You had seen him setting the examination hall ablaze; you had seen him giving speeches on the stage; you had seen him leaving everyone spellbound; you had seen him waving to the crowds of admirers, but somehow you couldn't see him come out with $E=mc^2$. I wonder whom to blame for all this! However, this boy rendered greater service than we ever expected of him when he entered the school."

"His grasping power, seriousness, desire to do the intangible, maintain healthy interactions with everyone, his sociability—everything was always indispensable to the school and would remain so for years to come. He always set high standards for others to emulate. He ruled for over six years and no one could ever wield him like a puppet."

"But talent cannot be kept hidden under wraps. It always comes out through some kind of medium and that is the body. Unfortunately the body has limited time period, irrespective of the amount of talent it has. The body is not immortal and finishes one day, but the talent of the body remains behind for people to remember it by keeping the person alive in their minds and in their hearts forever. I feel sorry to say that a person with such talent, a person with such veritable attitude, a person with umpteen skills, and a person with extreme passion is no longer among us. I have to say with profound sadness that Ayushman Agarwal—a student of 1998-2005 is no longer with us," said the principal, as his throat choked.

The principal's speech left everyone sad and crestfallen as they stood with their heads bowed. However, they only knew one thing about him and it was that they had lost him forever.

For some days, life at the school seemed to have lost its zing as everything seemed dull and quiet. Some took longer to recover from the depression caused by Ayushman's untimely death and some took seconds to forget all this since they had to put a leash on their feelings and get back to work. The school was sad but it had to get ready to receive the new batch of students waiting to join. A few months later, things returned to normal as though nothing had ever happened. Housemasters/housemistresses were back to their houses, the teachers to their teaching, sports, debates and prayer while the principal was back on his chair.

But memories of Ayushman remain forever. He would always remain there and would always help students and those who had helped amd loved him, for they would see him wandering around the campus.

I too left the school.

"So, do you have courage left to start this novel again?" I leave you with this question until I find some other Ayushman Agarwal. Now, if you think that Ayushman left a mark on your life, if you think that he held you spellbound, if you think he really taught you something and if you humbly think that he would always remain alive in your hearts, then go by what he used to say, "Either you exalt or you plummet; either you sit on the sun or sleep on the moon. Do whatever you want, but set a touchstone which would last forever. Do something which would immortalise your name."

Beyond Love

By Ankit Uttam

Price	:	Rs. 125
Pages	:	224
Size	:	5.0×7.75 inches
Binding	:	Paperback
Language	:	English
Subject	:	Fiction/Romance
ISBN	:	9788183520126

About the book:

If you think that MITs, IIMs and IITs are the be all and end all of the every college.

THEN THINK AGAIN...

Get ready for a roller coaster ride in the coolest college of the country because this year your definitions will take an about-turn and on this highway many romantic hearts will be shattered. Be ready to experience a war between your mind and your heart, for that four letter CUSS word...........LOVE.

Love is not always pure, sacrifice, friendship, cupid, red, saintly or simply a four letter word. Discover the darkest secrets of your heart where love deciphers into lust, betrayal, money, blasphemy, destruction, war, death, evil, myth and a question.

A tale of four and a half love stories and a hell lot of disaster which should not have happened and unfortunately it did happen.

Discover what the hell lies beneath and beyond those four letter word......LOVE?

Just Friends...

By Sumrit Shahi

Price	:	Rs. 99
Pages	:	264
Size	:	5.0×7.75 inches
Binding	:	Paperback
Language	:	English
Subject	:	Fiction/Romance
ISBN	:	9788183520119

National Bestseller

About the book:

He knows everything about her, right from her favourite books to her favourite bra.
She knows everything about him, right from his favourite soccer club to his favourite x rated websites.
He will complete her English homework, even at three in the night.
She will arrange an Armani suit for him, even if it calls for flirting with ugly guys.
He has her picture in his wallet.
She has his number on speed dial.
They talk to each other all the time.
They talk about each other when they don't talk to each other.
They discuss everything from periods to playstation.
They have tasted alcohol and then thrown up...*together.*
They have bunked countless tuitions... *together.*
They can't live without each other.
YET
They don't love each other.
They are **JUST FRIENDS...**

'Just Friends' is funny, honest, sad and straight from the heart.

—The Indian Express

Through his debut novel, Sumrit tries to reflect the mindset of a teenager and the relationship shared between the modern day parents and their children.

—The Hindustan Times

That's the Life Baby

By Priyesh Ranjan

Price	:	Rs. 99
Pages	:	224
Size	:	5.0×7.75 inches
Binding	:	Paperback
Language	:	English
Subject	:	Fiction/Romance
ISBN	:	9788183520003

National Bestseller

About the book:

Sixteen is sweet, Seventeen sweeter and Eighteen is the sweetest!

He thinks so.

What about Love at Eighteen? It happens, everyday! Doesn't it?

True for him!

Have a lot of girls in your life. It feels macho to have options. Girls don't need the advice. They are the wiser sex and have been playing *multi-boying* games for eons.

.....But he has three gorgeous damsels, all envious and shooting high testosterone levels.

How will you thank god if your balcony faces a girls' hostel? .....By being there 24X7? May be!

Exactly what he aims at!

Skirts lead to scandals. Don't they? Ban it or allow scandals.

He loves both, skirts and scandals.

What does he think about 'committed' tag?

You can't keep on eating the same chocolate all the time! Feels like jailed!!!

Meet Abhi. He is one of you with a devil's head! A year at Kota and his life remains no more the same. It all starts with a Bollywood-style love at first sight with Aditi. He sees, he falls, he cajoles and a little luck makes them one! Together they write new rules of dating & romance. Their amorous adventures will make you feel the passion of adolescence. But one day everything changes. How? What? Why? Answers lie in the story.

A stormy honeymoon of emotions......Get ready to laugh and cry!!!

Trust Me, it'll Work!!

By Mohit Naryani

Price	:	Rs. 125
Pages	:	240
Size	:	5.0 x 7.75 inches
Binding	:	Paperback
Language	:	English
Subject	:	Fiction/Romance
ISBN	:	9788183520836

About the book:

If you really want to kill yourself, don't get drunk before that.

However badly you decide, you can't fight your own destiny (sure you can deal with it, especially when girls around are fighting for liquor).

If you want to kill your sweet girlfriend's insane best friend, don't wait up for the break up; chances are that you could get stuck with both.

You might be obsessed with finding out a reason to why you broke up with someone, especially when they come in front of you in minimal clothing.

Sometimes life doesn't give you what you deserve, but not in the case of Rahul. In his case it happens only all the time, be it his bright future in the field or a romantic linkup with an angel!! And in those desperate times he is left with no choice but to lend his soul to the Satan, Teesha aka Tish (of course, in human form). Will they be able to overcome an overprotective Dad and a hot-shot businessman? Find out what all Rahul has to go through to get his true love via the cynicism of Tish.

The Promise

By Chital Mehta

Price	:	Rs. 125
Pages	:	240
Size	:	5.0×7.75 inches
Binding	:	Paperback
Language	:	English
Subject	:	Fiction/Romance
ISBN	:	9788183520133

About the book:

Dad says, 'Go to work' (how boring!)

Heart says, 'Have a blast' (yippee)

Dad kicks me out. What do I do now? (Lost!)

Friends are damn busy (Grrrrrrr)

I meet Pinky (It's definitely love at first sight, believe me!)

I join CAT class (whoa! I am in love)

My love life rolls on rocking (yeah, she loves me too. Great na?)

Dad is also happy (Son is finally studying. Duh!)

Rani steps in….nice girl, really cute (just a friend!)

She is my best friend but then…she says she loves me…

Oops… I kiss her (I didn't mean to…)

But I love Pinky (Do I?)

And I have made her a promise… (I can't break it)

This is me, Ajay. (Lost and confused madly in love)

Can you really measure friendship and love?

Step into Ajay's world which is filled with frolic, fun, confusions and craziness to discover the truth about friendship and love.

Dear, I Love You

By Arun Sabtharishi

Price	:	Rs. 125
Pages	:	208
Size	:	5.25 x 7.75 inches
Binding	:	Paperback
Language	:	English
Subject	:	Fiction/Romance
ISBN	:	9788183520874

About the book:

A guy sees a girl, falls in love…woos and wins her love. They both experience the ecstasy of love that develops between them and both realise the purport of love. They discover that love is blind, literally blind against anything in the world. The guy makes a mistake; he seeks forgiveness from the girl. The girl too commits a mistake. Again the guy seeks apologies from her. Does the girl forgive the guy modestly for the mistake SHE has made?

Beyond just hormone secretion or the chemical reaction that takes place in the human body, love is something more. Trust...hope...life...

This is a story of love, affection, bliss, blues, hassles and harmony between a guy and his girl when both are forced to acknowledge, "Dear, I love you!"